# 先知
## The Prophet

（英汉对照本）

〔黎巴嫩〕纪伯伦（Kahlil Gibran）　著

罗益民　译

河南人民出版社

**图书在版编目（CIP）数据**

先知＝The Prophet ：英汉对照本／（黎巴嫩）纪伯伦（Kahlil Gibran）著；罗益民译． — 郑州 ：河南人民出版社，2022. 4
ISBN 978 - 7 - 215 - 13039 - 5

Ⅰ．①先…　Ⅱ．①纪…　②罗…　Ⅲ．①散文诗 - 诗集 - 黎巴嫩 - 现代 - 英、汉　Ⅳ．①I378.25

中国版本图书馆 CIP 数据核字（2022）第 059521 号

河南人民出版社 出版发行

（地址：郑州市郑东新区祥盛街 27 号 邮政编码：450016 电话：65788077）
新华书店经销　　　　　河南瑞之光印刷股份有限公司印刷
开本　880毫米×1230毫米　　　1/32　　　印张　7.5
字数　126 千字
2022 年 4 月第 1 版　　　　　2022 年 4 月第 1 次印刷

定价：39.99 元

The Prophet

by

Kahlil Gibran

2004

(140th printing)

New York: Alfred A. Knopf

# 译序

　　《先知》已是家喻户晓的名作，且有著名作家冰心的名译。按理说，再来一个译本，不是画蛇添足，也是狗尾续貂。那为什么还明知故犯，做这种多余的事情呢？第一个原因，可能是因为译者太喜欢原作的文字和其中的美了。约在20世纪90年代，译者购得湖南文艺出版社出版的十种英汉对照世界十大诗人的抒情诗选集，它们包括莎士比亚、弥尔顿、彭斯、华兹华斯、雪莱、惠特曼等英美诗人的诗集，有两位是来自非本土英语世界的诗人，一位是印度的泰戈尔，一位是黎巴嫩诗人纪伯伦。他们虽然不是本土的英语诗人，但他们的创作是用英语写成或自己译出的。英美诗人的英语土生土长，不用说，肯定是非常地道的，但对于非英语世界的学习者来说，更有距离感；而就泰戈尔和纪伯伦这样自己的母语是非英语的诗人，他们的创作更加具有规范性，因此，更加适合非英语世界英语学习和英语使用的人的心意。因而，泰戈尔和纪伯伦读起来，对于中国人来说，更加亲切，更加"可口"。可能是因为这一点，增加了读者的喜爱度。也可能因为这一点，非英语国家的读者尝到了甜头，看见了希望，自然更爱读，也就更加深入人心了。

我读两位诗人的诗歌，不是从译文开始的，是在掌握了一定程度的英语以后开始的，所以更有亲切感，读起来基本没有障碍。在夜幕降临之后，青灯烛影素帐之下，捧卷而读，是一种莫大的享受。在飞越大洋的航班上，在大洋彼岸的日日夜夜，纪伯伦的《先知》《沙与沫》，泰戈尔的《园丁集》，都是我爱不释手的书卷。再后来，就有一试拙笔、动用管毫之心，想要自己翻译这些脍炙人口的诗行。这事一旦上手，就欲罢不能了。另外，之所以如此，在潜在的意识里，我想，一定是想要与人分享。

这些年来，从自己学习英语，到执教杏坛三十年，因为学习的本行是外语和它背后的文学，自然就和翻译这个行当脱不了干系。虽然我的主业是文学阅读和文学研究，为此攻读了英语文学的博士学位，后来再攻下来的是哲学博士学位，但翻译仍然是义不容辞的己任。我翻译了一些英文的短篇小说，汉语的短诗，白居易的长诗《长恨歌》(电子工业出版社,2020年),之前还写了一些翻译研究方面的论文,甚至还招收翻译方向的硕士、博士生,再加上和翻译家以及翻译界学者的交往,渐渐喜欢上翻译尤其是文学翻译这样一件事情。所以,翻译异国文字,就成了一件自然而然的事情了。

另一个使我动了"凡心",要着手翻译纪伯伦的这部诗集的理由可能是众人认为的第一重要理由。那就是对已有的译本不甚满意。之所以这不是我首要的理由,是因为,第一,文学作品我不主张读译本。可能我小时候译本读得少,反倒成为一个益处。这使我觉得,译本和原作的距离必须最小才最好。在我读了以对照形式附有冰心译本的原文之后,我发现译本和原作有出入,尤其是原作的韵味、节奏,特别是音乐素质方面的东西,不能和原文很好地吻合起来。我的自译之心就萌动了。第二,有幸和翻译家、编辑家、莎士比亚学者苏福忠先生认识,在长达二十年的交往中,一些常人认为的既成定论的看法改变了。比如,我以前崇尚的一些名家的译文,后来在事实上发现的确有或多或少的问题存在,且与世人认为的看法不一致。对于这些问题,心里如有鲠在喉,由于未及解决,因此常觉不快。苏先生是在出版社编辑翻译作品数十年的人,他见过多种译文,他探索过多种

3

译例的得失，最后他总结出检测译文的基本标准，他把它们概括为四个 M：meaning（意义），information（信息），message（隐义）和 image（形象），即在基本意义、上下文、隐含意义以及综合意义方面的既分又合的意义总和。新批评学派使用的 tension 一词本义是"内涵"和"外延"的总和。从某种程度上说，这四个 M 也同样算是对新批评概念 tension 的进一步具体化解释。这些因素在语法上都是名词，表明是翻译过程中涉及的必不可少的因素，较之严复的"信、达、雅"更为具体化。从理解和操作角度来看，"达"是"信"的补充和提高，反过来，"信"也是"达"的进一步完善。"雅"，则是指文言文的修辞和修养，对白话文构不成一个翻译标准；正因如此，"信、达、雅"也历来引起了不少的争议，且总是众说纷纭、不得要领。如果按照苏先生的考察体系，"信"和"达"是内容和意义方面的要求，"雅"则应归于白话文的文体和风格方面的要求，即文通字顺。"信"这个标准不仅是中国译学界公认的共识，也是世界范围内的无可非议的看法。所谓意大利谚语暗示出的背叛说，广为传诵的美国诗人弗罗斯特所说到的丢失理论（诗歌就是翻译中丢失的部分。——大意，译者注。），西方盛行的等效翻译理论，其实都是"信"的原则的变种。但是，怎样才能"信"，如何又能"达"，这也是很不容易弄清楚的问题。20世纪30年代，英国诗人、新批评理论家燕卜荪的名作《多重复义的七种类型》，虽然是一部文学批评的论著，却表明诗歌文本意义的复杂性。在翻译中，尤其是诗歌翻译中，如何把握他发现的这七种多重复义呢？这是一个一直困扰文学理论家、批评家和翻译理论家的难题。如果按照等效翻译理论的总结，严复的"信"和"达"是成立的，也是很有见地的。换一句话说，人们往往把"信"理解为索绪尔所说的所指（the Signified）方面的意义，不包括语言在声音和符号等方面即能指（the Signifier）的特点。也正是因为这个特点，人们对翻译过程中应该执行的标准参数就有遗漏，也因为如此，译者听从理论家和读者的这种"呼声"，就不能在事实上做到最大程度上、最大可能地忠实（"信"）于原文和原作。而且，在读者见不到或者不懂原文的情况下，再加上读者既定的具有潜涉抑制作用的母语习惯，译者讨好译本读者的口味，就可以掩盖译者对原作翻译的缺失和舛误。事实上，之所以要读译作，正是因为见不到原作或读不懂原文，这是翻译存在的基本理由。不仅如此，由于理论逻辑上把"信"的概念和"达"以及"雅"的概念分开，由于有时候偏重于强调后二者，就对在"信"的方面犯下的错误大有纵容和包庇之嫌。虽然"雅"不属于现代文即白话文适合的标准，但它业已成为认识上的一种无法去除的看法，因而也常常为人所利用。比如主张音形意美的理论，就与严复的理论有相通之处。不仅如此，由于翻译所涉及的因素的复杂性，在翻译理论和研究方面也出现了众说纷纭的局面。比如，在音形意美理论方面，就有人公然主张，在翻译中找不到对等词的时候，"就要尽可能选用优于原文的表达方式"（许渊冲：《梦与真：许渊冲自述》。河南文艺出版社，2017 年，第 003 页），而且，在这种理论看来，文学翻译尤其如此。这样说，就是明目张胆地违背了"信"的认识传统。这样就从一个角度打破了翻译理论中最高也是最基本的一个原则，即忠实的原则。译本读者读的时候有心理上的期待视界，即译作多大程度上转换了或反映了原作的包括一切可能在内的信息。事实上，在文体等方面的信息也在"信"和忠实的范围内，而且，这也是所有翻译理论在常识和基本逻辑上达成的共识。所谓"以韵害意"，正是没有用于描写翻译研究但事实上见于翻译实际操作中的一个现象。反过来说，有韵如果没有体现出来，同样违背了忠实（即"信"）这个基本原则。韵可以看成是对文本音乐素质的一种具体化和狭义的概括和表述，总而言之，这里所说的韵，是音乐素质的一种微缩。推而广之，它就是文体。文体同样应该被包括在"信"这个原则之中。如果失去了这一点，或者在这方面做得不好，那就表现为译作的质量问题。从原作的角度看，越是能够传神或者相像的表达，越可以认为是好的译作。在原作和译作作为两端的天平上，越是平衡越是达到了译者和读者的理想，二者的转换和交流过程中的损失便越小。正因为这个忠实和平衡的关系，加上本诗集的译者二十年来教授外语和翻译的习惯，才推动译者操刀试笔，翻译这部脍炙人口的世界名著。

翻译是一件极其有难度的事情。任何译品要保证高质量，甚至不被人诟病或挑剔，都是极难做到的。因此，译者也不想借此机会臧否前译，弘扬本译。好坏优劣，有心的读者自有公论。更重要的是，这里的译作是和原作并置的，正误可以自明。因此，读者可以自己去判断。另外，纪伯伦是世界知名的诗人。关于他的生平、艺术品格、价值、关怀的话题，都属于常识性的问题，也有书可查，有卷可翻，不需要在这里赘言。前述的英汉对照本《纪伯伦抒情诗选》(湖南文艺出版社，1996 年)就有冰心二女婿北京外国语大学陈恕教授的长篇介绍文字。再者，诗集《先知》本身已经赫然摆在读者的面前，可以敞开心扉去体味和品尝。

这部诗集动工翻译是近十年前的事情，一直想找个中意的出版社，也出于其他的一些考虑，至今才与河南人民出版社有出版的缘分。感谢译文编辑室主任刘玉军先生玉成。他向来对文学、莎士比亚的支持，是功在千秋的。没有他，难有这样一个译本问世。在翻译和修改的过程中，不少朋友提供了这样那样的帮助，比如，苏福忠先生、袁帅亚博士、刘伯弢先生、吴冬月女士、罗峰博士、刘伴博士等。特别需要提及的是苏先生和袁博士，前者对我在翻译方面的耳濡目染，锱铢讨论，使我受益无穷。先生至少通读过两次译稿。可以说，他是我翻译方面的具有现实主义性质的指导老师。我们也是被他戏称的莎士比亚的哼哈二将，互相支持，彼此砥砺。这对这部诗集的翻译也有间接但很实际的促进意义。袁博士在整个诗集的通读和细节方面提出的问题，让我避免了诸多可能出现的错误，这里特别加以感谢。同时也感谢我昔日的同窗好友刘伯弢，我们之间点点滴滴的讨论，对我帮助不小。我还要感谢的是朱法荣教授，她不辞辛劳，通读全书，详细校对，并为本书写了读后感，置于书后，大有蓬荜生辉之感。同时，这样做对理解诗人的作品亦有帮助。我还要特别感谢的是《英语世界》和当时的主编魏令查先生，选了其中五篇，刊发于彼。这说明了对所译文字的认可。特别是这些篇什的编辑赵岭老师，功夫炉火纯青，令我赞叹和佩服，我也从中学到了不少东西，同时保证了译作的质量。感谢责任编辑徐昊老师的辛勤工作，才使拙译如期面世。但不管怎么说，文责自负，译作中存在的问题，都希望并欢迎读者指出，以便帮助提高。《文心雕龙》"序志篇"说："生也有涯，无涯惟智。"这正合了古希腊时候就有的谚语：Life is short, but art is long. 但愿作为艺术的使者，诗歌的翅膀，可以给读者一些不同的想象和美。也用《文心雕龙》同一出处的两句话来结束我的《序言》："文果载心，余心有寄。"

译者

2021 年 7 月 6 日于巴山缙麓梦坡斋，

2021 年 7 月 9 日于巴山缙麓梦坡斋修订，

2022 年 2 月 26 日于巴山缙麓梦坡斋终定。

Contents
目 录

1

The Prophet

先知

# The Coming of the Ship

Almustafa[1], the chosen and the beloved, who was a dawn onto his own day, had waited twelve years in the city of Orphalese for his ship that was to return and bear him back to the isle of his birth.

And in the twelfth year, on the seventh day of Ielool, the month of reaping, he climbed the hill without the city walls and looked seaward; and he beheld the ship coming with the mist.

Then the gates of his heart were flung open, and his joy flew far over the sea. And he closed his eyes and prayed in the silences of his soul.

But as he descended the hill, a sadness came upon him,

---

1 阿拉伯男子常用名，意为"先知"。

# 航船到了

　　艾勒一穆斯塔法，上帝的选民，受到爱戴之人，时代的曙光，在奥菲利斯城里待了十二年，等待他的航船，把他送回到他出生的小岛。

　　在第十二个年头里，伊路尔收获月[1]的第七天，他爬上城墙外的小山，眺望大海；他看见航船从迷雾中驶来。

　　他的心扉被訇然打开，心中的欢乐漂洋过海，飞向远方。他闭上双眼，在灵魂的静默中祈祷。

　　可是当他走下小山，忽然悲从中来，他在心中默想：

---

1　伊路尔收获月：犹太历六月，相当于公历八九月间。

and he thought in his heart:

How shall I go in peace and without sorrow? Nay, not without a wound in the spirit shall I leave this city.

Long were the days of pain I have spent within its walls, and long were the nights of aloneness; and who can depart from his pain and his aloneness without regret?

Too many fragments of the spirit have I scattered in these streets, and too many are the children of my longing that walk naked among these hills, and I cannot withdraw from them without a burden and an ache.

It is not a garment I cast off this day, but a skin that I tear with my own hands. Nor is it a thought I leave behind me, but a heart made sweet with hunger and with thirst.

Yet I cannot tarry longer.

The sea that calls all things unto her calls me, and I must embark.

For to stay, though the hours burn in the night, is to freeze and crystallize and be bound in a mould.

Fain would I take with me all that is here. But how shall I?

我怎么能心平气静地离开而不留下忧伤呢？不，我不会不带着心灵的伤痛离开这座城市。

多少个漫长痛苦的白日，我在它的城墙内备受煎熬；多少个漫漫孤寂的夜晚，我再难打发。谁能告别自己的痛苦和寂寞而没有遗憾？

我把数不清的精神的碎片撒满了街巷；我无以计数的渴望的孩子赤身露体地在山间行走；没有负担，没有伤痛，我是无法从他们中间脱身的。

今天，不是一件外衣我要脱下，而是一层肌肤，要我亲手撕掉。也不是我抛诸脑后的思想，而是一颗心，因为饥渴而甜美。


可我不能再等了。

召唤万物的大海也在召唤我，我必须启航。

因为，虽然时光在夜里燃烧，踟蹰便会结成冰，便会晶体般变硬，然后在铸模当中禁锢起来。

我多想把这里的一切都带走，可是怎么带走呢？

A voice cannot carry the tongue and the lips that give it wings. Alone must it seek the ether.

And alone and without his nest shall the eagle fly across the sun.

Now when he reached the foot of the hill, he turned again towards the sea, and he saw his ship approaching the harbour, and upon her prow the mariners, the men of his own land.

And his soul cried out to them, and he said:

Sons of my ancient mother, you riders of the tides,

How often have you sailed in my dreams. And now you come in my awakening, which is my deeper dream.

Ready am I to go, and my eagerness with sails full set awaits the wind.

Only another breath will I breathe in this still air, only another loving look cast backward,

And then I shall stand among you, a seafarer among seafarers.

And you, vast sea, sleepless mother,

声音带不走赋予它双翅的唇舌。它必须自己寻找太空。

孤独的，失去巢穴的鹰就该飞越太阳。


这会儿当他来到了小山脚下，他回转身，再次眺望大海，看见海船驶向港湾，船头站满了水手，和他家乡的同胞。


他的灵魂冲着他们高喊，他说：

我祖母的儿孙啊，你们这些弄潮的人儿，

多少次你们在我的梦中航行！现在你们来了，在我梦醒的时候，可这是我更深沉的梦幻！

我已整装待发，我急切的心已经扬帆，只欠东风把它们舒展。

噢，让我再吸一口这宁静的空气，再含情脉脉地回望一眼，

然后我要站在你们的中间，成为水手中的水手！

你啊，无穷的大海，不眠的母亲！

Who alone are peace and freedom to the river and the stream,

Only another winding will this stream make, only another murmur in this glade,

And then shall I come to you, a boundless drop to a boundless ocean.


And as he walked he saw from afar men and women leaving their fields and their vineyards and hastening towards the city gates.

And he heard their voices calling his name, and shouting from the field to field telling one another of the coming of the ship.


And he said to himself:

Shall the day of parting be the day of gathering?

And shall it be said that my eve was in truth my dawn?

And what shall I give unto him who has left his plough in midfurrow, or to him who has stopped the wheel of his winepress?

Shall my heart become a tree heavy-laden with fruit that

你独自成为大河溪涧的安宁和自由，

这溪流再蜿蜒一次，再在林中空地呢喃一回，

我就朝你奔来，一颗无穷的水滴，奔入一片无垠的
汪洋。


正当他走着，他看见远处男男女女离开农田，离开
葡萄园，匆匆赶往城门口。

他听见他们叫他的名字，他们大声叫喊着，越过田野，
奔走相告，说接他的航船来了。


他对自己说：

难道离别的日子也会成为相聚的日子？

该不该说我的傍晚其实也就是我的黎明？

有人地耕了一半儿，就弃犁而去；有人停住榨葡萄的
机器，我该给他些什么？

难道我的心要变成一棵树，被果实压弯腰？让我可
以采摘下来赠与他们？

I may gather and give unto them?

And shall my desires flow like a fountain that I may fill their cups?

Am I a harp that the hand of the mighty may touch me, or a flute that his breath may pass through me?

A seeker of silences am I, and what treasure have I found in silences that I may dispense with confidence?

If this is my day of harvest, in what fields have I sowed the seed, and in what unremebered seasons?

If this indeed be the hour in which I lift up my lantern, it is not my flame that shall burn therein.

Empty and dark shall I raise my lantern,

And the guardian of the night shall fill it with oil and he shall light it also.


These things he said in words. But much in his heart remained unsaid. For he himself could not speak his deeper secret.


And when he entered into the city all the people came to meet him, and they were crying out to him as with one voice.

难道我的欲望要流成山泉，让我能够盛满他们的杯盏？

难道我是一张竖琴，神万能的手可以弹拨？或者一根长笛，他的气息可以穿过我的身体？

我是一个追求寂静的人，在我寻找到的寂静当中，可以找到什么样的宝贝儿，可以使我满怀信心地分发？

如果这是我的收获之日，在怎样的田野，在怎样的记不住的季节，我曾播下了种子？

如果这真是我提上灯笼的时刻，不应是我的火焰，该在其中燃烧。

四野空空，一片漆黑，我要举起灯笼，

更夫会给它加上燃油，还要把它点亮。


这些事儿他用话语说了出来，可还有很多都留在心中没有说，因为他自己是不可以说出更深的秘密的。


当他走进城里的时候，所有的人都来见他，他们大声对他说话，像是异口同声一般。

And the elders of the city stood forth and said:

Go not yet away from us.

A noontide have you been in our twilight, and your youth has given us dreams to dream.

No stranger are you among us, nor a guest, but our son and our dearly beloved. Suffer not yet our eyes to hunger for your face.


And the priests and the priestesses said unto him:

Let not the waves of the sea separate us now, and the years you have spent in our midst become a memory.

You have walked among us a spirit, and your shadow has been a light upon our faces.

Much have we loved you. But speechless was our love, and with veils has it been veiled.

Yet now it cries aloud unto you, and would stand revealed before you.

And ever has it been that love knows not its own depth until the hour of separation.

And others came also and entreated him. But he answered them not. He only bent his head; and those who

年长的市民站到前面说：

现在还不要离开我们。

在我们的黄昏里你度过了盛年，你把青春给了我们，让我们在梦里做梦。

在我们当中，你不是外人，也不是过客，而是我们的儿子，我们珍爱的人。不要让我们的双眼因渴求你的面孔而酸痛。


牧师们对他说：

还不要让海浪把我们分开，不要让你在我们当中的这些年成为一个记忆。

你曾在我们中间行走，像是一个精灵，你的影子成了我们脸上的光亮。

我们是多么地爱你！但无言的是我们的爱，它是用面纱罩住的。

可是现在，它大声地朝你喊叫，要褪去面纱，站在你面前。

事情总是这样，要是不到分别时刻，爱是不知道它自己的深度的。

其他人也来了，都来恳求他。可是他不作答，只是低下头，站得近的人看见他的泪，滴落到他的胸襟上。

stood near saw his tears falling upon his breast.

And he and the people proceeded towards the great square before the temple.


And there came out of the sanctuary a woman whose name was Almitra. And she was a seeress.

And he looked upon her with exceeding tenderness, for it was she who had first sought and believed in him when he had been but a day in their city.

And she hailed him, saying:

Prophet of God, in quest for the uttermost, long have you searched the distances for your ship.

And now your ship has come, and you must needs go.

Deep is your longing for the land of your memories and the dwelling place of your greater desires; and our love would not bind you nor our needs hold you.

Yet this we ask ere you leave us, that you speak to us and give us of your truth.

And we will give it unto our children, and they unto their children, and it shall not perish.

In your aloneness you have watched with our days, and

他和人们继续前行，来到寺庙前的广场上。


从神殿里走出一位女子，她的名字叫阿尔米特拉。
她是一位先知。

他异常温柔地打量她，因为她是在他第一天进城且
只待了一天的时候找到他并相信他的人。

她招呼他说：

神的先知，为了寻求无限，很长时间你都在寻找航
船的远近。

现在你的航船来了，看来你是非走不可了。

你对你记忆里的故乡的渴望，你对你更想去居住的
地方的渴望是那样的深；我们的爱不会束缚你，我们的
需要也不会抓住你不放。

可是在你离开以前，我们问你，请你说出来，说出你
知道的那些真理。

我们会把它传给我们的孩子，他们再传给他们的孩
子，它将永远流传，绵延不绝。

你在孤独中观察我们的白昼，你醒着的时候，你听
见我们在梦中啼笑。

in your wakefulness you have listened to the weeping and the laughter of our sleep.

Now therefore disclose us to ourselves, and tell us all that has been shown you of that which is between birth and death.

And he answered,

People of Orphalese, of what can I speak save of that which is even now moving your souls?

所以，现在把我们展示给我们自己吧，告诉我们展现给你的那一切生死之间的事情吧。


他回答说，

奥菲利斯的人民，除开那正在驱使你们的灵魂运行的东西，我还能说些什么呢？

# Love

Then said Almitra, Speak to us of Love. And he raised his head and looked upon the people, and there fell a stillness upon them. And with a great voice he said:

When love beckons to you follow him,

Though his ways are hard and steep.

And when his wings enfold you yield to him,

Though the sword hidden among his pinions may wound you.

And when he speaks to you believe in him,

Though his voice may shatter your dreams as the north wind lays waste the garden.

For even as love crowns you so shall he crucify you.

Even as he is for your growth so is he for your pruning.

Even as he ascends to your height and caresses your

# 爱情

　　阿尔米特拉说："你给我们说说爱情吧。"他抬起头，望着人们，他们突然鸦雀无声，一片寂静。随后他大声说：

　　爱向你召唤时，你就跟他而去吧，

　　哪怕他的路艰难，陡峭。

　　他展开翅膀，把你拥住，你便听从他摆布吧，

　　哪怕那把藏在他羽毛中的剑也许会伤着你。

　　他对你说话，你就相信他吧，

　　哪怕他的声音，会使你的梦破灭，正如北风会让花园成为一片荒芜。

　　因为正如爱情为你加冕王冠的时候，他也还会把你钉上十字架。正如他栽培你，他也还会把你修剪。

　　正如他爬到你的高处，抚慰你在阳光下震颤的最柔

tenderest branches that quiver in the sun,

So shall he descend to your roots and shake them in their

clinging to the earth.


Like sheaves of corn he gathers you unto himself.

He threshes you to make you naked. He sifts you to free

you from your husks.

He grinds you to whiteness.

He kneads you until you are pliant;

And then he assigns you to his sacred fire, that you may

become sacred bread for God's sacred feast.


All these things shall love do unto you that you may

know the secrets of your heart, and in that knowledge become

a fragment of Life's heart.


But if in your fear you would seek only love's peace and

love's pleasure,

Then it is better for you that you cover your nakedness

and pass out of love's threshing-floor,

Into the seasonless world where you shall laugh, but not

弱的枝条，

　　他也还会降到你的根部，摇晃你紧贴着大地的根茎。


　　像玉米捆一样，他把你收集到自己的身上。

　　他把你脱粒，让你赤身露体。他用筛子筛你，让你从壳儿中解脱出来。

　　他把你磨成白色的粉末。

　　他搓揉你，把你变软；

　　然后他把你架到他的圣火上，让你变成神的圣餐中神圣的面包。


　　爱做这一切，是为了让你能知晓你心的秘密。在这当中，你变成了生命之神的心的碎片儿。


　　可是如果你只在害怕时你才想寻求爱的安宁和爱的愉悦，

　　那么，你最好还是把赤裸的身体遮盖起来，走出爱的脱粒场，

　　走进没有季节的世界，在那里放声欢笑，可那不是

all of your laughter, and weep, but not all of your tears.

Love gives naught but itself and takes naught but from itself.

Love possesses not nor would it be possessed;

For love is sufficient unto love.

When you love you should not say, "God is in my heart," but rather, "I am in the heart of God."

And think not you can direct the course of love, if it finds you worthy, directs your course.

Love has no other desire but to fulfil itself.

But if you love and must needs have desires, let these be your desires:

To melt and be like a running brook that sings its melody to the night.

To know the pain of too much tenderness.

To be wounded by your own understanding of love;

And to bleed willingly and joyfully.

To wake at dawn with a winged heart and give thanks

你全部的欢笑，你将哭泣，但那也不是你全部的泪水。

爱只把自己献出，除了自己从不索取。
爱不占有，也不让人占有；
因为爱是自足的。

你爱的时候不要说，"神在我心里，"而要说，"我在神的心里。"
如果爱发现你的价值，指引你的行程，不要认为，你就可以操纵爱的方向。

除了完善自己，爱没有别的奢求。
但若你爱，你便定会有欲望，让以下这些成为你的欲望吧：
融化自己，做一条奔流的小溪，把美妙的旋律唱给黑夜。
认识痛苦，那是过多的温柔。
从自己对爱的理解中得到伤害；
心甘情愿，兴高采烈地流血。
清晨醒来，心带着翅膀，为又一天的爱说声感谢；

for another day of loving;

    To rest at the noon hour and meditate love's ecstasy;

    To return home at eventide with gratitude;

    And then to sleep with a prayer for the beloved in your

heart and a song of praise upon your lips.

在正午时分休息片刻，想想爱的眩晕；

傍晚回家的时候，带着感激；

上床安歇时，在心中为心爱的人祷告，张开嘴，唱一首赞美的歌。

# Marriage

Then Almitra spoke again and said, And what of Marriage, master?

And he answered saying:

You were born together, and together you shall be forevermore.

You shall be together when white wings of death scatter your days.

Aye, you shall be together even in the silent memory of God.

But let there be spaces in your togetherness,

And let the winds of the heavens dance between you.

Love one another but make not a bond of love:

Let it rather be a moving sea between the shores of your souls.

# 婚姻

阿尔米特拉又开口说:"大师,那婚姻是怎么回事儿呢?"

他回答说:

你们一起出生,也会永远在一起。

即使死亡白色的羽翼,把你们的日子拆得七零八落,你们也应在一起。

是啊,即使在安静地回想神的时刻里,你们也会在一起。

但你们在一起的时候,也要留有空间,

让天堂的风,在你们之间舞动。


彼此相爱,但不要订什么爱的盟约:

让它成为你们灵魂的海岸之间流动的海洋。

Fill each other's cup but drink not from one cup.

Give one another of your bread but eat not from the same loaf.

Sing and dance together and be joyous, but let each one of you be alone,

Even as the strings of a lute are alone though they quiver with the same music.


Give your hearts, but not into each other's keeping.

For only the hand of Life can contain your hearts.

And stand together, yet not too near together:

For the pillars of the temple stand apart,

And the oak tree and the cypress grow not in each other's shadow.

相互斟满杯盏，但不要只喝同一杯水。

彼此互赠面包，但不要只吃同一块面包。

一起歌唱，一起舞蹈，充满欢乐，但让每个人都独立生活，

正如诗琴震颤出同样的音乐，它们的弦却是各自分开的。


把心交给对方，但勿进入对方的保留地。

因为只有生命之神之手，才能容纳你的心。

站在一起，但别靠得太近：

因为寺庙里的柱子是分开的，

橡树、柏树不在对方的阴影中成长。

# Children

And a woman who held a babe against her bosom said, Speak to us of Children.

And he said:

Your children are not your children.

They are the sons and daughters of Life's longing for itself.

They come through you but not from you,

And though they are with you, yet they belong not to you.

You may give them your love but not your thoughts.

For they have their own thoughts.

You may house their bodies but not their souls,

For their souls dwell in the house of tomorrow, which you cannot visit, not even in your dreams.

# 子女

一位怀抱着婴儿的妇女说："给我们讲讲子女吧。"

他说：

你们的子女不是你们自己的。

他们是生命之神的渴望自身的儿女。

他们经你的身体而来，却不从你的身上分出来，

虽然跟你在一起，却不属于你。

你可以把你的爱给他们，你的思想却给不了，

因为他们有他们自己的思想。

你可以把他们的身体庇护起来，却庇护不住他们的灵魂，

因为他们的灵魂居住在明天的房子里，即便是在梦

You may strive to be like them, but seek not to make them like you.

For life goes not backward nor tarries with yesterday.

You are the bows from which your children as living arrows are sent forth.

The archer sees the mark upon the path of the infinite, and He bends you with His might that His arrows may go swift and far.

Let your bending in the archer's hand be for gladness;

For even as he loves the arrow that flies, so He loves also the bow that is stable.

中，你也是无法拜访的。

你可以努力学他们的样子，但千万不要让他们像你。

因为，生命无法倒退，也无法与往昔同在。

你是弓，孩子们是从你身上射出的活生生的箭。

弓箭手瞄准无边小径上的目标，他用神力让你弯曲，好让那箭射得又快又远。

让你的弯曲在弓箭手手里成为他的欢乐；

因为正如它热爱飞逝的箭，神也热爱那稳健的弓。

# Giving

Then said a rich man, Speak to us of Giving.

And he answered:

You give but little when you give of your possessions.

It is when you give of yourself that you truly give.

For what are your possessions but things you keep and guard for fear you may need them tomorrow?

And tomorrow, what shall tomorrow bring to the overprudent dog burying bones in the trackless sand as he follows the pilgrims to the holy city?

And what is fear of need but need itself?

Is not dread of thirst when your well is full, thirst that is unquenchable?

There are those who give little of the much which they have—and they give it for recognition and their hidden desire

# 给予

然后一位富豪说:"给我们说说给予吧。"

他回答说:

你把拥有的东西拿出来,你并未给人什么。

你把自己奉献出来,那才是真正的给予。

你拥有的东西,难道不就是因害怕明天需要而存起来看守着的那些东西吗?

明天,明天会给那过于小心翼翼的狗带来什么,他随着香客去圣城朝拜,把骨头埋进茫茫的沙漠?

除开需求本身,对需求的恐惧是什么?

你井满之时你仍害怕口渴,难道不是这样一种口渴是止不住的吗?


有些人有很多给出的却很少,他们给出来是为了认可,他们见不得人的欲望,让他们的礼物失去了美好。

makes their gifts unwholesome.

And there are those who have little and give it all.

These are the believers in life and the bounty of life, and their coffer is never empty.

There are those who give with joy, and that joy is their reward.

And there are those who give with pain, and that pain is their baptism.

And there are those who give and know not pain in giving, nor do they seek joy, nor give with mindfulness of virtue;

They give as in yonder valley the myrtle breathes its fragrance into space.

Through the hands of such as these God speaks, and from behind their eyes He smiles upon the earth.


It is well to give when asked, but it is better to give unasked, through understanding;

And to the open-handed the search for one who shall receive is joy greater than giving.

And is there aught you would withhold?

还有一些人，他们拥有的不多，却倾囊而出。

这些人是相信生活，相信生活是富足的，他们的储柜从来就没有亏空过。

有一些人，他们给得高高兴兴，高兴便是他们的回报。

有些人给得很痛苦，痛苦便是他们的洗礼。

有些人给予，从不知给予的痛苦，他们也从不寻求欢乐，也从不因在乎美德而给予；

他们给予，就像远处山谷里的桃金娘把香气吐进空中。

通过这些人的手，神说话了，在他们的眼睛背后，神朝着世人微笑。

要的时候给出固然很好，没有要的时候，只因心领神会而给，那就更好；

对于慷慨豪爽之人，给出去是快乐，找个人来接受则更快乐。

难道你是想把一切都攒在手里不放吗？

All you have shall some day be given;

Therefore give now, that the season of giving may be yours and not your inheritors'.


You often say, "I would give, but only to the deserving."

The trees in your orchard say not so, nor the flocks in your pasture.

They give that they may live, for to withhold is to perish.

Surely he who is worthy to receive his days and his nights is worthy of all else from you.

And he who has deserved to drink from the ocean of life deserves to fill his cup from your little stream.

And what desert greater shall there be than that which lies in the courage and the confidence, nay the charity, of receiving?

And who are you that men should rend their bosom and unveil their pride, that you may see their worth naked and their pride unabashed?

See first that you yourself deserve to be a giver, and an instrument of giving.

For in truth it is life that gives unto life—while you, who

你有的一切，总有一天都要给出去；

因此，不如现在就给出去，那么奉献的好时机便是你的，而不是你的继承人的。


你常说："我会解囊相赠，但只给值得的人。"

你园中的果树可不这么说，你牧场中的鸡鸭牛羊也不这么说。

它们给出，便可以活下来；攒在手里，便是自取灭亡。

毫无疑问，值得接受他的白天和黑夜的人，也就值得接受你给的这两样以外的所有东西。

值得从生命的大海中饮吸的人，也值得用你的涓涓溪流，斟满他的杯盏。

会有什么样的美德，可以胜过接受的勇气和信心，甚至接受的仁慈呢？

你是谁人？怎么值得别人对你敞开胸怀，揭开自尊的面纱，让你们看他们的价值赤裸着，让他们的自尊没有遮拦？

先看看你自己是否值得做一个奉献者，一个给予的工具吧。

说真的，是生命才给予了生命，而你，自以为是付出者，其实，只不过是个证人而已。

deem yourself a giver, are but a witness.

And you receivers—and you are all receivers—assume
no weight of gratitude, lest you lay a yoke upon yourself and
upon him who gives.

Rather rise together with the giver on his gifts as on
wings;

For to be overmindful of your debt, is to doubt his
generosity who has the free-hearted earth for mother, and God
for father.

而你们这些接受者——你们都是接受者——不要把感激看成负担，以免给你自己身上套上枷锁，或给给予者套上枷锁。

和给予者一起上升吧，升到他的赠物上，仿佛坐在羽翼之上；

因为，过于在乎债务，是怀疑其人的慷慨。然而，他有无私的地球作母，有神作父。

# Eating and Drinking

Then an old man, a keeper of an inn, said, Speak to us of Eating and Drinking.

And he said:

Would that you could live on the fragrance of the earth, and like an air plant be sustained by the light.

But since you must kill to eat, and rob the young of its mother's milk to quench your thirst, let it then be an act of worship,

And let your board stand an altar on which the pure and the innocent of forest and plain are sacrificed for that which is purer and still more innocent in many.

When you kill a beast say to him in your heart,

"By the same power that slays you, I too am slain; and I too shall be consumed.

For the law that delivered you into my hand shall deliver

# 饮食

然后，一位老人，一个小酒店的店主，说道："给我们说说饮食吧。"

他回答说：

要是你能靠地球的芳香生活，就像凤梨草靠阳光维持生命，那该多好！

然而，既然你为了吃就必须杀生，为了你自己解渴就抢走幼小动物的母乳，那么让它成为一个膜拜的行动吧。

还有，让你的餐桌上立个祭坛，把那些丛林里和原野上纯洁无害的物品，奉献给众多更为纯洁无邪的人。

你宰杀一头牲口的时候，请在心里对它说：

"我怎样以同样的力量杀害了你，也会被同样的力量杀掉；也会被同样的力量消耗干净。

因为你落在我手上依据的法则，也会把我传给一只

me into a mightier hand.

Your blood and my blood is naught but the sap that feeds the tree of heaven."


And when you crush an apple with your teeth, say to it in your heart,

"Your seeds shall live in my body,

And the buds of your tomorrow shall blossom in my heart,

And your fragrance shall be my breath,

And together we shall rejoice through all the seasons."


And in the autumn, when you gather the grapes of your vineyard for the winepress, say in you heart,

"I too am a vineyard, and my fruit shall be gathered for the winepress,

And like new wine I shall be kept in eternal vessels."

And in winter, when you draw the wine, let there be in your heart a song for each cup;

And let there be in the song a remembrance for the autumn days, and for the vineyard, and for the winepress.

44

更为强大的手。

你我的血液，不过是那喂养天堂之树的汁液。"


当你用牙齿嚼碎苹果的时候，请你在心里对它说：
"你的种子将活在我的体内，
你明天的花蕾将在我心中开放，
你的芳香将成为我的气息，
一年四季我们都将一起欢畅。"


同样，在秋天，你收摘葡萄，从葡萄园拿到榨酒机
的时候，在心里对它说：
"我也是一个葡萄园，我的果实也要收去拿给榨酒机，
还有，就像新酒一样，我也要存入永恒的容器里。"
冬天，你拿出酒来，每喝一杯，就在心里唱一首歌；
让这首歌记住秋天，记住葡萄园，记住榨酒机。

# Work

Then a ploughman said, "Speak to us of Work."

And he answered, saying:

You work that you may keep pace with the earth and the soul of the earth.

For to be idle is to become a stranger unto the seasons, and to step out of life's procession, that marches in majesty and proud submission towards the infinite.

When you work you are a flute through whose heart the whispering of the hours turns to music.

Which of you would be a reed, dumb and silent, when all else sings together in unison?

Always you have been told that work is a curse and labour a misfortune.

# 劳动

然后，一位耕夫说："跟我们讲讲劳动吧。"

他回答说：

你劳动，便可以和地球以及地球的灵魂保持同样的步伐。

因为，无所事事，你就成了四季的陌生人，走出了生活的队伍，无法威严而毕恭毕敬地挺进，走向无限。

劳动的时候，你是一枝长笛，时光的喁喁细语穿过你的心，变成了音乐。

你们谁愿变成一根芦苇，哑然无声，而其他所有的人则一起歌唱？

总是有人告诉你，劳动是诅咒，劳作是不幸。

But I say to you that when you work you fulfil a part of
earth's furthest dream, assigned to you when that dream was
born,

And in keeping yourself with labour you are in truth
loving life,

And to love life through labour is to be intimate with
life's inmost secret.


But if you in your pain call birth an affliction and the
support of the flesh a curse written upon your brow, then
I answer that naught but the sweat of your brow shall wash
away that which is written.


You have been told also life is darkness, and in your
weariness you echo what was said by the weary.

And I say that life is indeed darkness save when there is
urge,

And all urge is blind save when there is knowledge,

And all knowledge is vain save when there is work,

And all work is empty save when there is love;

And when you work with love you bind yourself to

我倒是要告诉你，你劳动了，地球最遥远的梦一旦诞生出来，分派给你，你便把这个梦的一部分变成了现实。

让自己一直劳作，才是真正地热爱生活，

通过劳作热爱生活，是和生活最深奥的秘密保持亲切。

但你如果在痛苦的时候，把生育叫做受罪，把维持肉体叫做写在额头上的诅咒，那么我告诉你，那正是你额头上的汗水，才能把那写在上面的东西洗掉。

也有人告诉你，生活就是黑暗，疲惫之中，你正好成为疲惫者的回音。

而且我要说，除开有渴望的时候，生活真的就是黑暗。

我还要说，除非有知识，所有的渴望，都是盲目的。

除非有劳动，所有的知识都是白费。

除非有爱，所有的劳动都是空虚。

你带着爱劳动，你便把自己与自己、自己与别人、自己与神合为一体了。

yourself, and to one another, and to God.

And what is it to work with love?

It is to weave the cloth with threads drawn from your heart, even as if your beloved were to wear that cloth.

It is to build a house with affection, even as if your beloved were to dwell in that house.

It is to sow seeds with tenderness and reap the harvest with joy, even as if your beloved were to eat the fruit.

It is to charge all things you fashion with a breath of your own spirit,

And to know that all the blessed dead are standing about you and watching.

Often have I heard you say, as if speaking in sleep, "he who works in marble, and finds the shape of his own soul in the stone, is a nobler than he who ploughs the soil.

And he who seizes the rainbow to lay it on a cloth in the likeness of man, is more than he who makes the sandals for our feet."

But I say, not in sleep but in the over-wakefulness of

那什么是有爱的劳动呢？

是织布的时候，让线从你的心里引出来，就好像你心爱的人要穿戴那布料做成的衣服。

是带着感情修一栋房舍，就好像你心爱的人就要住在这里面一样。

是带着柔情播下种子，带着欢乐收割庄稼，就好像你心爱的人们要吃下那些果实一样。

是让所有你创造的事物都充满你心灵的气息。

要知道：所有受到祝福的逝者都站在你身边看着你。


我经常听你梦呓般地说："跟大理石打交道的劳动者，在石头里发现他自己灵魂的形态，比那些犁地者要高尚许多。

以人的形象抓住了彩虹放在一块布上的人远远胜过为脚制作趿履之人。"

可是我要说，不是在睡梦中，而是在正午觉醒之时，

noontide, that the wind speaks not more sweetly to the giant oaks than to the least of all the blades of grass;

And he alone is great who turns the voice of the wind into a song made sweeter by his own loving.


Work is love made visible.

And if you cannot work with love but only with distaste, it is better that you should leave your work and sit at the gate of the temple and take alms of those who work with joy.

For if you bake bread with indifference, you bake a bitter bread that feeds but half man's hunger.

And if you grudge the crushing of the grapes, your grudge distils a poison in the wine.

And if you sing though as angels, and love not the singing, you muffle man's ears to the voices of the day and the voices of the night.

风对巨大无比的橡树说的甜蜜语言，并不比最卑微的草叶唱得更为动人。

独自把风的声音，变成一首因自己的爱更甜美的歌，他也是了不起的。


劳动是看得见的爱。

如果劳动无法带着爱，而只有恨，那不如放下手中的活儿，坐在庙门口，等待愉快地劳动的人们给予施舍。

因为如果心不在焉地烤面包，你烤的面包是苦涩的，只能止住半个人的饿。

如果榨葡萄的时候心中闷闷不乐，那么，你酿出来的酒，也充满了毒液。

即使你像天使一样唱歌，但并不热爱歌唱本身，你塞住了人们的耳朵，让他们无法听见白昼和黑夜的声音。

# Joy and Sorrow

Then a woman said, Speak to us of Joy and Sorrow.

And he answered:

Your joy is your sorrow unmasked.

And the selfsame well from which your laughter rises was oftentimes filled with your tears.

And how else can it be?

The deeper that sorrow carves into your being, the more joy you can contain.

Is not the cup that hold your wine the very cup that was burned in the potter's oven?

And is not the lute that soothes your spirit, the very wood that was hollowed with knives?

When you are joyous, look deep into your heart and you shall find it is only that which has given you sorrow that is giving you joy.

# 欢乐与忧愁

接下来一位女子说："跟我们说说欢乐与忧愁吧。"

他回答说：

你的欢乐是你不用面具罩起来的忧愁。

涌出了笑声的同一口井，也常常充满了泪水。

除此还能怎么样呢？

忧愁在你身上刻得越深，你身上装载的欢乐就越多。

你装着葡萄酒的杯子难道不就是制陶匠炉子里烧过的那只吗？

那把抚慰你心灵的诗琴不就是那根用刀掏空了的木头吗？

你兴高采烈的时候，窥探你心灵的深处，你会发现，给你带来了忧愁的，正好也正在给你带来欢乐。

When you are sorrowful look again in your heart, and you shall see that in truth you are weeping for that which has been your delight.

Some of you say, "Joy is greater than sorrow," and others say, "Nay, sorrow is the greater."

But I say unto you, they are inseparable.

Together they come, and when one sits alone with you at your board, remember that the other is asleep upon your bed.

Verily you are suspended like scales between your sorrow and your joy.

Only when you are empty are you at standstill and balanced.

When the treasure-keeper lifts you to weigh his gold and his silver, needs must your joy or your sorrow rise or fall.

你满怀忧愁的时候，再看看你心灵的深处，你会发现，其实那一直让你欢畅的，你正在为它哭泣。

　　你们当中有人说："欢乐比忧愁多。"其他人则说，"不！忧愁比欢乐多。"

　　但是我要对你们说，它们是无法分开的。

　　它们总是结伴而行。其中一个独自地和你坐在桌边的时候，可要记住：另一个正熟睡在你的床上。

　　事实上，你就像天平，吊在忧愁与欢乐之间摇摆不定。

　　只有当你空无一切的时候，你才能稳定、平衡。

　　管理财宝的司库抬举你，要你称他金银的重量，此时你该注意：你的欢乐或忧愁要沉浮变化了。

# Houses

Then a mason came forth and said, Speak to us of Houses.

And he answered and said:

Build of your imaginings a bower in the wilderness ere you build a house within the city walls.

For even as you have home-comings in your twilight, so has the wanderer in you, the ever distant and alone.

Your house is your larger body.

It grows in the sun and sleeps in the stillness of the night; and it is not dreamless. Does not your house dream? And dreaming, leave the city for grove or hilltop?

Would that I could gather your houses into my hand, and like a sower scatter them in forest and meadow.

Would the valleys were your streets, and the green

# 房子

然后一个石匠走上前来说："给我们说说房子吧。"

他回答说：

先在野外把你的各种想象修成凉亭，再在城墙内修房子吧。

因为就好像在黄昏时你要回家，你身上的那个流浪者要回家，他是那个一直遥远，孤身只影的人。

你的房子是你更大的躯壳儿。

它在阳光下成长，在夜的宁静里睡眠；它不是没有梦的。你的房子不做梦吗？它做着梦，离开城市，去找树林或者小山丘了吧？

假若我能把你们的房子收集在我手里，就像一个播种人，把它们撒进森林和草地，那该多好啊！

假若河谷是你们的大街，绿油油的小径是小巷，你

paths your alleys, that you might seek one another through vineyards, and come with the fragrance of the earth in your garments.

But these things are not yet to be.

In their fear your forefathers gathered you too near together. And that fear shall endure a little longer. A little longer shall your city walls separate your hearths from your fields.

And tell me, people of Orphalese, what have you in these houses? And what is it you guard with fastened doors?

Have you peace, the quiet urge that reveals your power?

Have you remembrances, the glimmering arches that span the summits of the mind?

Have you beauty, that leads the heart from things fashioned of wood and stone to the holy mountain?

Tell me, have you these in your houses?

Or have you only comfort, and the lust for comfort, that stealthy thing that enters the house a guest, and becomes a host, and then a master?

们就可以在葡萄园里相互造访，衣服里散发着泥土的芬芳，那该多好啊！

可是这些事情还没有变成现实。

因为惧怕，你们的祖先把你们安置得太近。这个惧怕会持续再长一点儿。城墙把你们的炉灶和你们的田地也会分隔得再远一点儿。


告诉我，你们这些奥菲利斯人，你们这些房子里有些什么？你们门户紧锁要保护的是什么？

你们有和平，有那显示你们的力量的平静的冲动吗？

你们有记忆，有那些横跨心灵的山峰之间那些光芒四射的拱桥吗？

你们有美，有那把心从草木顽石的形态牵引到圣山来吗？

告诉我，你们的房子里有这些吗？

要么你们只有舒适，对舒适的渴望，那个东西偷偷摸摸地进了房子，当了客人，变成主人，最后成了老爷？

Ay, and it becomes a tamer, and with hook and scourge makes puppets of your larger desires.

Though its hands are silken, its heart is of iron.

It lulls you to sleep only to stand by your bed and jeer at the dignity of the flesh.

It makes mock of your sound senses, and lays them in thistledown like fragile vessels.

Verily the lust for comfort murders the passion of the soul, and then walks grinning in the funeral.


But you, children of space, you restless in rest, you shall not be trapped nor tamed.

Your house shall be not an anchor but a mast.

It shall not be a glistening film that covers a wound, but an eyelid that guards the eye.

You shall not fold your wings that you may pass through doors, nor bend your heads that they strike not against a ceiling, nor fear to breathe lest walls should crack and fall down.

啊，它变成了驯服手，拿着挂钩和鞭子，把你们更大的欲望变成了玩偶。

虽然它纤手若丝，它的心却如铁石。

它把你哄睡着了，站在床边，讥笑你肉体的尊严。

它嘲笑你健全的意识，把它们放进蓟花的羽冠，就像放进易碎的器皿。

事实上，贪图安逸的渴望谋杀了灵魂的激情，然后在葬礼上，龇牙咧嘴，大笑前行。


可是你们，宇宙的孩子们，你们在休止中无休无止，你们不应被捕猎，更不应被驯服。

你们的房子不应是一个锚，而应是根桅杆。

它不应该是遮掩伤口的闪光的薄膜，应该是保护眼睛的眼帘。

不要收起翅膀，好从门缝之间挤过，也不要低着头，生怕撞着天花板，更不要害怕呼吸，担心万一墙裂了缝倾塌下来。

You shall not dwell in tombs made by the dead for the living.

And though of magnificence and splendour, your house shall not hold your secret nor shelter your longing.

For that which is boundless in you abides in the mansion of the sky, whose door is the morning mist, and whose windows are the songs and the silences of night.

不要住在死人为活人修建的坟墓里。

虽然气势恢宏，壮丽非凡，你的房子不会为你保守秘密，也不会为你的欲望遮风挡雨。

因为你身上无边无际的东西住在天空的大厦里，它的门是早晨的迷雾，窗户是夜晚的歌声和寂静。

# Clothes

And the weaver said, Speak to us of Clothes.

And he answered:

Your clothes conceal much of your beauty, yet they hide not the unbeautiful.

And though you seek in garments the freedom of privacy you may find in them a harness and a chain.

Would that you could meet the sun and the wind with more of your skin and less of your raiment,

For the breath of life is in the sunlight and the hand of life is in the wind.


Some of you say,  "It is the north wind who has woven the clothes to wear."

And I say, Ay, it was the north wind,

But shame was his loom, and the softening of the sinews

# 衣服

且说织布工说:"跟我们讲讲衣服吧。"

他回答道:

你大部分的美都被衣服遮住了,可是衣服却遮不住那不美的地方。

虽然你在衣服里寻找隐秘的自由,可能在其中你找到的是羁绊和锁链。

要是你们能让肌肤多见阳光,多让清风吹拂,少让衣服包裹,那该多好!

因为,生命的呼吸在阳光之中,生命的手在清风里面。


你们中有人说:"是北风编织了我们身上穿的衣服。"

而我要说,是,曾经是北风,

可羞愧是它的织布机,软化肌筋的是它的线。

was his thread.

And when his work was done he laughed in the forest.

Forget not that modesty is for a shield against the eye of the unclean.

And when the unclean shall be no more, what were modesty but a fetter and a fouling of the mind?

And forget not that the earth delights to feel your bare feet and the winds long to play with your hair.

活儿干完了，他就在森林中开怀大笑。

不要忘记，恭谦是一张盾牌，可以抵御不洁的眼睛。

不洁不复存在的时候，恭谦是什么？它不是心灵的脚镣和污垢吗？

不要忘记：地球乐于感受你的赤脚，柔风渴望戏耍你的头发。

# Buying and Selling

And a merchant said, Speak to us of Buying and Selling.

And he answered and said:

To you the earth yields her fruit, and you shall not want if you but know how to fill your hands.

It is in exchanging the gifts of the earth that you shall find abundance and be satisfied.

Yet unless the exchange be in love and kindly justice, it will but lead some to greed and others to hunger.

When in the market place you toilers of the sea and fields and vineyards meet the weavers and the potters and the gatherers of spices, —

Invoke then the master spirit of the earth, to come into your midst and sanctify the scales and the reckoning that weighs value against value.

# 买卖

一位商人说:"跟我们说说买卖吧。"

他回答说:

地球给你奉献果实,如果你只知道怎样填满你自己的双手,那你是不该要的。

你发现富饶又感到满足的时候,那是在交换地球的礼物。

要是不以爱、善良和公正来交换,那只能使一些人贪得无厌,而另一些人则饥肠辘辘。

你们这些劳苦之人,在大海里、田野上、葡萄园中劳作,现在在市场上和织工、陶匠、香料商聚集在一起,

祈求大地的主宰精灵,让它来到你们中间,让天平神圣,让价钱算得也神圣。

And suffer not the barren-handed to take part in your transactions, who would sell their words for your labour.

To such men you should say, "Come with us to the field, or go with our brothers to the sea and cast your net;

For the land and the sea shall be bountiful to you even as to us."

And if there come the singers and the dancers and the flute players, —buy of their gifts also.

For they too are gatherers of fruit and frankincense, and that which they bring, though fashioned of dreams, is raiment and food for your soul.

And before you leave the marketplace, see that no one has gone his way with empty hands.

For the master spirit of the earth shall not sleep peacefully upon the wind till the needs of the least of you are satisfied.

在你们的交易中，不要让那些两手空空的人来参与，不要让他们用空言来换取你们的辛劳。

对这样的人你们应该说，"和我们一起到田地里来，和我们的兄弟一起出海并撒下你的网；

因为大地和海洋对于你们来说，也会像对我们一样慷慨。"

如果歌唱家、舞蹈家和吹笛人来了，也把他们的礼物买下来。

因为他们也是采集果实和乳香的人，他们带在身边的，虽然形式是梦，却是你们灵魂的衣食。

你们离开市场以前，保证没有人空手而去。

因为大地的主宰精灵不会心安理得地睡在风上，除非你们最低微之人的需要也得到了满足。

# Crime and Punishment

Then one of the judges of the city stood forth and said, Speak to us of Crime and Punishment.

And he answered saying:

It is when your spirit goes wandering upon the wind,

That you, alone and unguarded, commit a wrong unto others and therefore unto yourself.

And for that wrong committed must you knock and wait a while unheeded at the gate of the blessed.

Like the ocean is your god-self;

It remains for ever undefiled.

And like the ether it lifts but the winged.

Even like the sun is your god-self;

It knows not the ways of the mole nor seeks it the holes of the serpent.

# 罪与罚

然后，一位市里的法官走上前来说："跟我们说说罪与罚吧。"

他回答说：

正是你的灵魂随风飘荡之时，

你孤独无人守护，对别人犯下罪行，于是也对自己也犯下了罪行。

因为犯下这样的罪行，你必须去敲幸福者的大门，必须在门外稍稍地等一会儿。


像大海一般的，是你的君子自我；

它永远保持纯洁。

跟太空一样，它只提携有翅膀的。

甚至像太阳一般的，是你的君子自我；

它不知道鼹鼠的去路，也不去寻找毒蛇的洞穴。

But your god-self does not dwell alone in your being.

Much in you is still man, and much in you is not yet man,

But a shapeless pigmy that walks asleep in the mist searching for its own awakening.

And of the man in you would I now speak.

For it is he and not your god-self nor the pigmy in the mist, that knows crime and the punishment of crime.


Oftentimes have I heard you speak of one who commits a wrong as though he were not one of you, but a stranger unto you and an intruder upon your world.

But I say that even as the holy and the righteous cannot rise beyond the highest which is in each one of you,

So the wicked and the weak cannot fall lower than the lowest which is in you also.

And as a single leaf turns not yellow but with the silent knowledge of the whole tree,

So the wrong-doer cannot do wrong without the hidden will of you all.

Like a procession you walk together towards your god-self.

可是你的君子自我也不单独住在你的存在里。

你身上多半还是人，你身上多半还不是人，

而是一个无形无状、矮小而微不足道的人在迷雾中沉睡着，行走着，他边走边寻找自己的觉醒。

我现在说说你身上人的那一部分。

因为，是他而不是君子自我或迷雾中的小人自我知道罪恶及其惩罚。


我经常听你们说，一个人犯了罪，就好像他不是你们中间的一个了，而是一个陌生人，一个突然闯进你们世界里的人。

可是我要说，正如圣人和正人君子无法超越你们每一个人身上的最高境界。

所以，恶人和弱者同样也不可能低于同样存在于你们身上的最低境界。

正如一片孤单的叶子，未经整棵大树的默许，是不能枯黄的。

所以，没有你们大家秘而不宣的允诺，罪人不可能胡作非为。

就像一个列队，你们一起行进，走向你们的君子自我。

You are the way and the wayfarers.

And when one of you falls down he falls for those behind him, a caution against the stumbling stone.

Ay, and he falls for those ahead of him, who though faster and surer of foot, yet removed not the stumbling stone.


And this also, though the word lie heavy upon your hearts:

The murdered is not unaccountable for his own murder,

And the robbed is not blameless in being robbed.

The righteous is not innocent of the deeds of the wicked,

And the white-handed is not clean in the doings of the felon.

Yea, the guilty is oftentimes the victim of the injured,

And still more often the condemned is the burden-bearer for the guiltless and unblamed.

You cannot separate the just from the unjust and the good from the wicked;

For they stand together before the face of the sun even as the black thread and the white are woven together.

And when the black thread breaks, the weaver shall look

你们既是路也是行路之人。

你们其中一个倒下，他为的是他背后的人，为了提醒他们有一块绊脚石。

是的，他也为他前面的人跌倒，他们走得快，步子也稳，但是没有把那块绊脚石搬走。


再有，虽然这话让你们心情沉重：

遭谋杀者并非对其被杀全无责任，

被劫之人并非对其被劫无可责难。

正派之人对于坏人坏事并非完全无辜，

手上白白净净的人在残暴的行为中未必清白。

是啊，有罪之人常常是受伤害者的牺牲品。

更有甚者，受谴责的人常常为无罪无责的人背上负担。

正义与非正义，善与恶你是无法分开的。

因为，在太阳底下，它们是并肩站在一起的，就好像黑线和白线交织在一起一样。

当黑线断掉之时，织工应该看看那整块布料，他还应该检查一下织布机。

into the whole cloth, and he shall examine the loom also.

If any of you would bring judgment the unfaithful wife,

Let him also weigh the heart of her husband in scales, and measure his soul with measurements.

And let him who would lash the offender look unto the spirit of the offended.

And if any of you would punish in the name of righteousness and lay the ax unto the evil tree, let him see to its roots;

And verily he will find the roots of the good and the bad, the fruitful and the fruitless, all entwined together in the silent heart of the earth.

And you judges who would be just,

What judgment pronounce you upon him who though honest in the flesh yet is a thief in spirit?

What penalty lay you upon him who slays in the flesh yet is himself slain in the spirit?

And how prosecute you him who in action is a deceiver and an oppressor,

Yet who also is aggrieved and outraged?

你们不论是谁，如果把一个不守妇道的妻子拿来审判，

也让他把她丈夫的心拿到天平秤上来称一下，用尺子量量他的灵魂。

抽打犯事者之人，也让他审视一下受害者的心灵。

如果你们当中任何一位以正义的名分惩罚，把斧头架在罪恶之树上，让他看看它的根；

事实上，他会发现，善与恶，结有果实的和不结果实的，在地球默默不语的深处，它们都是纠缠在一起的。

你们这些应该胸怀正义的法官啊，

虽然肉体诚实可信，骨子里却是一个盗贼，这样的人你如何宣判？

残害了肉体，在精神上却遭到别人的残害，这样的人该如何定罪？

行为上的骗子、压迫者，同时为受了屈辱和被施行暴举的人，

你如何起诉他？

And how shall you punish those whose remorse is already greater than their misdeeds?

Is not remorse the justice which is administered by that very law which you would fain serve?

Yet you cannot lay remorse upon the innocent nor lift it from the heart of the guilty.

Unbidden shall it call in the night, that men may wake and gaze upon themselves.

And you who would understand justice, how shall you unless you look upon all deeds in the fullness of light?

Only then shall you know that the erect and the fallen are but one man standing in twilight between the night of his pigmy-self and the day of his god-self,

And that the corner-stone of the temple is not higher than the lowest stone in its foundation.

已经悔恨很深，甚至超过了他们的恶行，这些人你们该如何惩罚呢？

悔恨不就是正好被你们心甘情愿遵守的法律施行的正义吗？

然而你不能把悔恨放在无辜者的身上，也不能从有罪之人的心里拿走。

在夜晚，不受人点拨，人们就会醒来，仔细打量自己。

你们想要理解正义的，要不是在全然的光亮中审视一切行为，你们怎样去理解正义？

只有那时你们才知道，矗立起来的和倒下的只不过是同一个人，他站在夜晚的小人自我和白天的君子自我之间黄昏的微光中，

寺庙角落上的石头不会比它地基上最底下的石头高出多少。

# Laws

Then a lawyer said, But what of our Laws, master?

And he answered:

You delight in laying down laws,

Yet you delight more in breaking them.

Like children playing by the ocean who build sand-towers with constancy and then destroy them with laughter.

But while you build your sand-towers the ocean brings more sand to the shore,

And when you destroy them, the ocean laughs with you.

Verily the ocean laughs always with the innocent.

But what of those to whom life is not an ocean, and man-made laws are not sand-towers,

But to whom life is a rock, and the law a chisel with which they would carve it in their own likeness?

# 法律

一位律师说："可是我们的法律又怎么样呢，大师？"

他回答说：

你们喜欢制定法律，

不过你们更喜欢违背法律。

就跟在大海边玩耍的孩子一样，孜孜不倦地在沙滩上建起高楼，然后又哈哈大笑，把它们毁掉。

可是当你在沙滩上建起高楼的时候，大海向岸边送来了更多的沙，

当你毁掉它们的时候，大海也和你一起哈哈大笑。

其实大海总是和无辜的人一起欢笑。


可是对于那些生活不是大海的人来说又怎么样呢？

人为制定的法律不是沙滩上的高楼？

对于那些生活是顽石的人来说，法律是凿子，用它他们在岩石上雕刻和自己相像的形象？

What of the cripple who hates dancers?

What of the ox who loves his yoke and deems the elk and deer of the forest stray and vagrant things?

What of the old serpent who cannot shed his skin, and calls all others naked and shameless?

And of him who comes early to the wedding-feast, and when over-fed and tired goes his way saying that all feasts are violation and all feasters law-breakers?

What shall I say of these save that they too stand in the sunlight, but with their backs to the sun?

They see only their shadows, and their shadows are their laws.

And what is the sun to them but a caster of shadows?

And what is it to acknowledge the laws but to stoop down and trace their shadows upon the earth?

But you who walk facing the sun, what images drawn on the earth can hold you?

You who travel with the wind, what weathervane shall direct your course?

What man's law shall bind you if you break your yoke

残腿的人痛恨舞蹈家怎么办？

牛喜欢枷轭，认为森林里的麋鹿走错了路就是无业游民又该怎么办？

假如老蛇无法脱皮，就说所有其他裸着身子的都不知道害臊，又当如何？

提早到了婚宴之人，吃得过多，筋疲力尽，边走边说，所有宴会都是违法的，所有的赴宴者都是违法者，又当如何？


他们站在阳光下，却只能背对着太阳，对于这种情况除了这些我还能说什么呢？

他们只看见自己的影子，他们的影子就是法律。

对于他们来说，除开一个影子的投射者，太阳又是什么呢？

承认法律，只是要弯下腰查看他们在地球上的影子，这之外是什么？

可是，你面对太阳走路，画在地球上的什么样的图像可以管着你？

你和风一起旅行，什么样的风向标可以为你指引行程？

如果你砸碎枷锁，不冲破任何人的牢房，什么样人

but upon no man's prison door?

What laws shall you fear if you dance but stumble against no man's iron chains?

And who is he that shall bring you to judgment if you tear off your garment yet leave it in no man's path?

People of Orphalese, you can muffle the drum, and you can loosen the strings of the lyre, but who shall command the skylark not to sing?

为的法律可以约束你？

如果你跳舞，不撞破任何人的锁链，你会惧怕什么
样的法律呢？

如果你扯下衣衫，不丢弃在任何人的路上，那个把
你送上审判台的人又是谁呢？

奥菲利斯的人啊，你可以把鼓蒙住，可以把诗琴的
弦松开，谁又能命令云雀，不让它歌唱呢？

# Freedom

And an orator said, Speak to us of Freedom.

And he answered:

At the city gate and by your fireside I have seen you prostrate yourself and worship your own freedom,

Even as slaves humble themselves before a tyrant and praise him though he slays them.

Ay, in the grove of the temple and in the shadow of the citadel I have seen the freest among you wear their freedom as a yoke and a handcuff.

And my heart bled within me; for you can only be free when even the desire of seeking freedom becomes a harness to you, and when you cease to speak of freedom as a goal and a fulfillment.


You shall be free indeed when your days are not without

# 自由

一个演说家说："跟我们讲讲自由吧。"

他回答道：

在城门边，在炉火旁，我看见你匍匐在地，敬拜你自己的自由，

正如奴隶在暴君面前作践自己，就是杀了他们，他也赞美这位暴君。

是啊，在寺庙的小树林里，在城堡的阴凉处，我看见你们当中最自由的人把自由当成枷锁和手铐穿戴在身上。

我的心在我体内流血；因为只有当且仅当寻求自由的欲望对你也变成羁绊的时候，当你不再说自由是一种目标和成就的时候，你才可以自由。

当你白天并非没有焦虑，夜晚并非没有需求和悲伤，

a care nor your nights without a want and a grief,

But rather when these things girdle your life and yet you rise above them naked and unbound.


And how shall you rise beyond your days and nights unless you break the chains which you at the dawn of your understanding have fastened around your noon hour?

In truth that which you call freedom is the strongest of these chains, though its links glitter in the sun and dazzle the eyes.


And what is it but fragments of your own self you would discard that you may become free?

If it is an unjust law you would abolish, that law was written with your own hand upon your own forehead.

You cannot erase it by burning your law books nor by washing the foreheads of your judges, though you pour the sea upon them.

And if it is a despot you would dethrone, see first that his throne erected within you is destroyed.

你就真正自由了，

而且当这些事情束缚住你的生活，你还赤身露体，无拘无束地超越它们，你就真正自由了。

你早晨的理解之链锁住了你的正午时光，要是不挣断这些锁链你怎样超越白天和黑夜呢？

说真的，你叫做自由的东西是这当中最结实的锁链，即使它的扣子在阳光下闪闪发光，照得你头晕目眩。

仅仅是你自我的碎片你想丢弃，为的是你可以变得自由，这又是什么呢？

假如是一条不正义的法律，你想废除，而那法律却是你亲手写在自己的前额上的。

你无法靠焚烧法律典籍把它抹掉，纵使你决东海之波，也无法洗刷掉法官前额上的条文。

如果你想推翻一个暴君，首先要确保在你身上建立起来的王位给毁掉。

For how can a tyrant rule the free and the proud, but for a tyranny in their own freedom and a shame in their own pride?

And if it is a care you would cast off, that care has been chosen by you rather than imposed upon you.

And if it is a fear you would dispel, the seat of that fear is in your heart and not in the hand of the feared.


Verily all things move within your being in constant half embrace, the desired and the dreaded, the repugnant and the cherished, the pursued and that which you would escape.

These things move within you as lights and shadows in pairs that cling.

And when the shadow fades and is no more, the light that lingers becomes a shadow to another light.

And thus your freedom when it loses its fetters becomes itself the fetter of a greater freedom.

除非是因为自己的自由而施行暴政，因为自己的高傲而不顾荣辱，一个暴君怎样统治自由而不受管教的人？

如果你想丢掉一个焦虑，而它又是你自己选择而不是强加在你身上的，你该怎么办？

如果你想消除一种惧怕，那根基在你心里，而不在害怕的东西手里，你又当如何？


事实上，万事万物都在你的存在中运行，它们都永远半推半就地相互拥抱着，有的渴望拥有，有的惧怕拥有；有的避之不及，有的视若珍宝；有的趋之若鹜，有的避之惶惶。

这些东西在你的体内运行，正如光影相随，粘在一起。

当影子消失无存之时，光不住地流连，变成了另外一道光的影子。

所以你的自由失去羁绊的时候，就变成更大的自由的羁绊。

# Reason and Passion

And the priestess spoke again and said, Speak to us of Reason and Passion.

And he answered saying:

Your soul is oftentimes a battlefield, upon which your reason and your judgment wage war against passion and your appetite.

Would that I could be the peacemaker in your soul, that I might turn the discord and the rivalry of your elements into oneness and melody.

But how shall I, unless you yourselves be also the peacemakers, nay, the lovers of all your elements?

Your reason and your passion are the rudder and the sails of your seafaring soul.

If either your sails or your rudder be broken, you can but

# 理智与激情

女教士又开口说："跟我们讲讲理智与激情吧。"

他回答说：

你的心灵常常是一个战场，理智和判断向你的激情和欲望挑起战争。

但愿我能做一个你灵魂的和平的使者，把你的种种元素的不和谐和对立因素变成统一和旋律，

要是你自己也不是和平的缔造者，不仅如此，又热爱所有那些元素，我又有什么办法呢？

理智和激情是你远航的灵魂的舵和帆。

舵或者是帆，只要其中一个出了问题，你就只有漂来荡去，无法前行，要么就只有停滞在大海中央。

toss and drift, or else be held at a standstill in mid-seas.

For reason, ruling alone, is a force confining; and passion, unattended, is a flame that burns to its own destruction.

Therefore let your soul exalt your reason to the height of passion; that it may sing;

And let it direct your passion with reason, that your passion may live through its own daily resurrection, and like the phoenix rise above its own ashes.


I would have you consider your judgment and your appetite even as you would two loved guests in your house.

Surely you would not honour one guest above the other; for he who is more mindful of one loses the love and the faith of both.


Among the hills, when you sit in the cool shade of the white poplars, sharing the peace and serenity of distant fields and meadows—then let your heart say in silence, "God rests in reason."

And when the storm comes, and the mighty wind shakes the forest, and thunder and lightning proclaim the majesty of

因为，只有理智孤军奋战的话，是一种禁锢的力量；而激情在没有人管束的情况下，是把自己燃烧殆尽的火焰。

所以，让你的心灵把理智提高到激情的高度，它便可以歌唱；

让它用理智指挥激情，你的激情便可以通过它日复一日地复活获得新生，正如凤凰从自己的灰烬中站立起来。


我希望你们把判断和欲望甚至视为你们家中两位受爱戴的客人。

当然，对客人你不要厚此薄彼，认为一个在另一个之上；因为偏重一方，则会同时失去二者的友爱和信任。


在小山丘之中，你坐在白杨树凉爽的树荫下，分享着远处田野和草地带来的祥和与宁静，那么让你的心默默地说："神在理智之中栖息。"

暴风骤雨一来，狂风大作，摇撼着森林，雷鸣电闪，宣扬天空的威严，此时，让你的心怀着敬畏说："神在激情之中运行。"

the sky, —then let your heart say in awe, "God moves in passion."

And since you are a breath in God's sphere, and a leaf in God's forest, you too should rest in reason and move in passion.

在神的领地里，你是一丝气息；在神的森林里，你是一片叶子，因此，你也在理智中栖息，在激情里运行。

# Pain

And a woman spoke, saying, "Tell us of Pain."

And he said:

Your pain is the breaking of the shell that encloses your understanding.

Even as the stone of the fruit must break, that its heart may stand in the sun, so must you know pain.

And could you keep your heart in wonder at the daily miracles of your life, your pain would not seem less wondrous than your joy;

And you would accept the seasons of your heart, even as you have always accepted the seasons that pass over your fields.

And you would watch with serenity through the winters of your grief.

Much of your pain is self-chosen.

# 痛苦

一位女子开口说:"跟我们讲讲痛苦吧。"

他说:

你的痛苦就是敲碎包含你理解的蛋壳儿。

正如果实的核仁必须破碎,它的心才能在阳光下傲然屹立,所以,你必须认识痛苦。

如果日常生活中的奇迹使你心里感到诧异,你的痛苦便也像你的快乐一样神奇了;

你会接受你心的四季,就像你总是那样习以为常地接受翻越你田野的四季一样。

你要静静地守望,以度过你悲凉的冬季。

你多数的痛苦都是自己选择的。

It is the bitter potion by which the physician within you heals your sick self.

Therefore trust the physician, and drink his remedy in silence and tranquillity:

For his hand, though heavy and hard, is guided by the tender hand of the Unseen,

And the cup he brings, though it burn your lips, has been fashioned of the clay which the Potter has moistened with His own sacred tears.

正是那苦涩的汁液，你体内的医生用它治愈了你患病的自我。

所以，相信医生吧，把他给的药剂静静地、心平气和地喝下去：

因为他的手虽然又厚又硬，却被那只看不见的柔软的手引导着，

他拿来的杯子，虽然烫嘴，却是那位陶匠用他自己神圣的泪水调湿的黏土做成的。

# Self-Knowledge

And a man said, "Speak to us of Self-Knowledge."

And he answered, saying:

Your hearts know in silence the secrets of the days and the nights.

But your ears thirst for the sound of your heart's knowledge.

You would know in words that which you have always known in thought.

You would touch with your fingers the naked body of your dreams.

And it is well you should.

The hidden well-spring of your soul must needs rise and run murmuring to the sea;

And the treasure of your infinite depths would be

# 自知

一位男子说:"跟我们讲讲自知吧。"

他回答说:

你的心在静默中领悟白天和黑夜的秘密。

可你的耳朵渴望倾听关于你心的知识的声音。

你想通过文字知道你一直在思想里知道的东西。

你想用你的手指触摸梦幻的光光的身子。

你就应该这样做。

你灵魂里潜伏着的井泉一定想要升上来,呢喃着奔向大海;

你无尽头的深处的宝藏会暴露给你的眼睛。

revealed to your eyes.

But let there be no scales to weigh your unknown treasure;

And seek not the depths of your knowledge with staff or sounding line.

For self is a sea boundless and measureless.


Say not, "I have found the truth," but rather, "I have found a truth."

Say not, "I have found the path of the soul." Say rather, "I have met the soul walking upon my path."

For the soul walks upon all paths.

The soul walks not upon a line neither does it grow like a reed.

The soul unfolds itself, like a lotus of countless petals.

可是别让天平去称你那无人知晓的宝藏；

别用标杆或绳子去检测你知识的深度。

因为，自我是无边的海，是无法测量的。

不要说"我已找到了真理"，而要说"我找到了一条真理"。

不要说"我找到了灵魂之路"，而要说"灵魂在我的路上行走，我碰见了它"。

因为灵魂在所有的路上行走。

灵魂不在一条直线上行走，也不像一根芦苇那样成长。

灵魂把自己展开，就像荷莲，有无数的花瓣。

# Teaching

Then said a teacher, Speak to us of Teaching.

And he said:

No man can reveal to you aught but that which already lies half asleep in the dawning of our knowledge.

The teacher who walks in the shadow of the temple, among his followers, gives not of his wisdom but rather of his faith and his lovingness.

If he is indeed wise he does not bid you enter the house of wisdom, but rather leads you to the threshold of your own mind.

The astronomer may speak to you of his understanding of space, but he cannot give you his understanding.

The musician may sing to you of the rhythm which is in all space, but he cannot give you the ear which arrests the rhythm nor the voice that echoes it.

# 教学

然后一位教师说："跟我们讲讲教学吧。"

他说：

除开业已半睡半醒地躺在知识的晨曦之中的，谁也不能向你揭示什么。

行走在寺庙的阴影之中，和他的追随者一起的老师，给的不是他的智慧，而是他的信仰和怜爱。

倘若他真的很明智，他便不会让你走进智慧的殿堂，而是领你走向你自己心灵的门槛。

天文学家可能会向你说起他对太空的理解，可是他给不了他的理解。

音乐家可以对你唱充满太空的节奏，但他给不了捕捉节奏的耳朵以及回应那回音的嗓子。

And he who is versed in the science of numbers can tell of the regions of weight and measure, but he cannot conduct you thither.

For the vision of one man lends not its wings to another man.

And even as each one of you stands alone in God's knowledge, so must each one of you be alone in his knowledge of God and in his understanding of the earth.

谁精通数字的科学，就可以讲说重量和尺度的领域，可是他无法引领你走向那里。

因为，一个人的视野不可能假另一人以它的翅膀。

正如你们每个人都单独站立在神的知识当中，你们每个人对于神的认识，对于世界的理解也一定是独立的。

# Friendship

And a youth said, Speak to us of Friendship.

And he answered, saying:

Your friend is your needs answered.

He is your field which you sow with love and reap with thanksgiving.

And he is your board and your fireside.

For you come to him with your hunger, and you seek him for peace.


When your friend speaks his mind you fear not the "nay" in your own mind, nor do you withhold the "ay."

And when he is silent your heart ceases not to listen to his heart;

For without words, in friendship, all thoughts, all desires, all expectations are born and shared, with joy that is unacclaimed.

# 友谊

一个年轻人说:"跟我们讲讲友谊吧。"

他回答说:

你的需要得到了回应,那就是朋友。

他是一片田野,你带着爱播种,带着感激收获。

他是你的餐桌,是你的壁炉。

肚子饿了,你就来找他;想安宁了,你就来找他。

你的朋友说起心事儿,在你的心里你不怕"不"字,你也不吝啬一个"是"字。

他沉默不语的时候,你的心一直听着他的心语,从不停下。

因为,就友谊来说,不需要用语言,所有的思想、欲望、期望都产生和分享,带着不需言明的欢乐。

When you part from your friend, you grieve not;

For that which you love most in him may be clearer in his absence, as the mountain to the climber is clearer from the plain.

And let there be no purpose in friendship save the deepening of the spirit.

For love that seeks aught but the disclosure of its own mystery is not love but a net cast forth: and only the unprofitable is caught.


And let your best be for your friend.

If he must know the ebb of your tide, let him know its flood also.

For what is your friend that you should seek him with hours to kill?

Seek him always with hours to live.

For it is his to fill your need, but not your emptiness.

And in the sweetness of friendship let there be laughter, and sharing of pleasures.

For in the dew of little things the heart finds its morning and is refreshed.

你和朋友分别的时候，你不忧伤；

因为，他身上你最爱的东西，也许在他不在的时候更加清楚，就像登山者看山在平地上看得更清楚一样。

除非为了让精神更为深邃，友谊不要有别的目的。

因为只寻求揭露自身秘密的爱不是爱，而只是撒下的一张网，网住的都是些毫无用处的东西。

把你最好的东西给你的朋友吧。

倘若他一定要知道你退潮时候的情况，让他也知道你涨潮时候的情况。

因为如果你仅仅是因为度日如年需要找他消磨时光，那算什么朋友？

找他总是要为了充实地生活。

因为，是他的时光填满了你的需要，而不是你的空虚。

在友谊的甜美中，让它有欢畅的笑声，把愉快分享。

因为，在微不足道的事物的露珠当中，心找到了清晨，再一次焕发出了青春。

# Talking

And then a scholar said, Speak of Talking.

And he answered, saying:

You talk when you cease to be at peace with your thoughts;

And when you can no longer dwell in the solitude of your heart you live in your lips, and sound is a diversion and a pastime.

And in much of your talking, thinking is half murdered.

For thought is a bird of space, that in a cage of words may indeed unfold its wings but cannot fly.


There are those among you who seek the talkative through fear of being alone.

The silence of aloneness reveals to their eyes their naked selves and they would escape.

And there are those who talk, and without knowledge or forethought reveal a truth which they themselves do not

# 说话

一位学者说："跟我们讲讲说话吧。"

他回答说：

你不再与你的思想和睦相处的时候你便说话；

你无法在你心灵的孤寂中住下来的时候，你就住在嘴上，声音是转移注意力，是消磨时光。

在你多数的谈话中，思想被谋杀了一半。

因为思想是空中之鸟，在文字的牢笼中，也许真能展开翅膀，却无法飞翔。

你们当中某些人，因为害怕孤独，才找饶舌的人说话。

孤寂把他们赤裸的自我暴露给他们的眼睛，他们想逃避。

有些人说话，既没有知识，又没有先见，揭示出一条真理，就连他们自己也不懂是什么。

understand.

And there are those who have the truth within them, but they tell it not in words.

In the bosom of such as these the spirit dwells in rhythmic silence.

When you meet your friend on the roadside or in the market place, let the spirit in you move your lips and direct your tongue.

Let the voice within your voice speak to the ear of his ear;

For his soul will keep the truth of your heart as the taste of the wine is remembered.

When the colour is forgotten and the vessel is no more.

还有一些人，他们自己就有真理，但他们不用文字说出来。

在这些人的胸中，精神住在有节奏的无言中。

在路边上或市场上遇见朋友，让精神来移动你的嘴唇，指挥你的舌头吧。

让你声音中的声音对他耳朵的耳朵说话吧；

因为他的灵魂会守住你心中的真理。

当颜色被遗忘，杯子也不复存在的时候，酒的味道仍然会被记住。

# Time

And an astronomer said, Master, what of Time?

And he answered:

You would measure time the measureless and the immeasurable.

You would adjust your conduct and even direct the course of your spirit according to hours and seasons.

Of time you would make a stream upon whose bank you would sit and watch its flowing.


Yet the timeless in you is aware of life's timelessness,

And knows that yesterday is but today's memory and tomorrow is today's dream.

And that that which sings and contemplates in you is still dwelling within the bounds of that first moment which scattered the stars into space.

# 时间

一位天文学家说:"大师,那时间呢?"

他回答说:

你想度量没有限度、无法度量的时间。

你想按照钟点和四季调整你的行为,指引你精神的方向。

你想把时间做成一条溪流,坐在岸上,看着它流淌。

然而,你身上的无限意识到生命也是无限的,

它知道昨天只不过是今天的记忆,明天是今天的梦。

它也知道,在你体内歌唱和默想的,现在仍然住在你原初的境界里,而在当时,它把星星撒进了太空。

Who among you does not feel that his power to love is boundless?

And yet who does not feel that very love, though boundless, encompassed within the centre of his being, and moving not from love thought to love thought, nor from love deeds to other love deeds?

And is not time even as love is, undivided and spaceless?

But if in your thought you must measure time into seasons, let each season encircle all the other seasons,

And let today embrace the past with remembrance and the future with longing.

你们当中谁没有感觉到爱的力量是无穷的？

然而谁没有感觉到，那个爱尽管无限，却包含在他存在的中心，不是从一个爱的思想移动到另一个爱的思想，从一些爱的行动移动到其他爱的行动？

正如爱是无法分割、没有空间的，难道时间不也是这样吗？


可是如果在你的思想中你必须把时间度量为四季，那就让每一个季节围绕着其他季节吧，

让今天用记忆拥抱过去，用渴望拥抱未来吧。

# Good and Evil

And one of the elders of the city said, Speak to us of Good and Evil.

And he answered:

Of the good in you I can speak, but not of the evil.

For what is evil but good tortured by its own hunger and thirst?

Verily when good is hungry it seeks food even in dark caves, and when it thirsts, it drinks even of dead waters.

You are good when you are one with yourself.

Yet when you are not one with yourself you are not evil.

For a divided house is not a den of thieves; it is only a divided house.

And a ship without rudder may wander aimlessly among perilous isles yet sink not to the bottom.

# 善恶

一位年长的市民说："跟我们讲讲善与恶吧。"

他回答说：

你身上的善我可以说，恶我说不了。

因为恶不就是被它自身的饥渴折磨着的善么？

事实上，当善饥饿之时，哪怕在黑暗的山洞，它也要寻找食物；当它焦渴了，即便是脏水也要喝。

你和你的自我同一之时你就善良。

可是当你和你的自我不在一体的时候，你也不邪恶。

因为分隔了的房宅不是贼窝；它只是分开了的房舍。

没有舵的航船可能会漫无目的地在危险的小岛之间漂流，但不至于会沉入水底。

You are good when you strive to give of yourself.

Yet you are not evil when you seek gain for yourself.

For when you strive for gain you are but a root that clings to the earth and sucks at her breast.

Surely the fruit cannot say to the root, "Be like me, ripe and full and ever giving of your abundance."

For to the fruit giving is a need, as receiving is a need to the root.


You are good when you are fully awake in your speech,

Yet you are not evil when you sleep while your tongue staggers without purpose.

And even stumbling speech may strengthen a weak tongue.


You are good when you walk to your goal firmly and with bold steps.

Yet you are not evil when you go thither limping.

Even those who limp go not backward.

But you who are strong and swift, see that you do not limp before the lame, deeming it kindness.

你努力把自己献出的时候，你是善良的。

但当你为自己追逐利益的时候，你也不是邪恶的。

因为当你为利益挣扎的时候，你不过是一条根须，紧紧地抓住大地，在她胸前吮吸。

毫无疑问，果实不能对根说："像我一样，成熟、丰盈，永不停息，把你的富饶奉献出来。"

因为对于果实来说，给予是一种必要，就像接受对于根来说是一种必要一样。


你发表演说的时候，如果完全清醒，那你是善良的，

可是当你睡着了的时候，你的舌头漫无目的地打转，你也不是邪恶的。

甚至结结巴巴地演说，也会使一个柔弱的舌头力量倍增。


当你迈着坚定而大胆的脚步走向你目标的时候，你是善良的。

然而当你步履蹒跚地走过去的时候，你也不是邪恶的。

即便那些人跛着脚，也不走回头路。

可是你们那些强壮而且身子灵活的人，注意不要在残腿的人面前跛足而行，还把它当作友好。

You are good in countless ways, and you are not evil when you are not good,

You are only loitering and sluggard.

Pity that the stags cannot teach swiftness to the turtles.


In your longing for your giant self lies your goodness: and that longing is in all of you.

But in some of you that longing is a torrent rushing with might to the sea, carrying the secrets of the hillsides and the songs of the forest.

And in others it is a flat stream that loses itself in angles and bends and lingers before it reaches the shore.

But let not him who longs much say to him who longs little, "Wherefore are you slow and halting? "

For the truly good ask not the naked, "Where is your garment? " nor the houseless, "What has befallen your house? "

你的善是说不完道不尽的，当你不善之时你也不邪恶。

你只是在闲逛，懒懒散散混日子。

很遗憾鹿无法教乌龟变得敏捷。


在你渴望的巨大的自我中，存有你的善良：那种渴望你们每一个人身上都有。

可是对你们当中有些人来说，渴望是湍急的洪流，奋力冲向大海，携着山坡的秘密和林木的歌唱。

对另一些人来说，它是平缓的溪流，转弯抹角，失去自我，走走停停，最后才到达海边。

可是不要让渴望强烈的对愿望微弱的说："为什么如此慢慢吞吞，踟蹰不前啊？"

因为，真正善良的不会问没有穿衣服的人说："你的衣服呢？"也不会问没有房子住的人："你的房子怎么啦？"

# Prayer

Then a priestess said, Speak to us of Prayer.

And he answered, saying:

You pray in your distress and in your need; would that you might pray also in the fullness of your joy and in your days of abundance.

For what is prayer but the expansion of yourself into the living ether?

And if it is for your comfort to pour your darkness into space, it is also for your delight to pour forth the dawning of your heart.

And if you cannot but weep when your soul summons you to prayer, she should spur you again and yet again, though weeping, until you shall come laughing.

When you pray you rise to meet in the air those who are

# 祷告

一位女教士说："跟我们讲讲祷告吧。"

他回答说：

你悲伤，有需要的时候祷告；要是你满心快乐的时候或者在富裕的日子里也祷告那该多好。

因为，除开把自己扩展、延伸到生命的天国，还有什么是祷告？

如果你是为了把你自己的暗夜倾倒进太空才感到舒服的话，那么你把心灵的晨曦倾倒出来也是愉快的。

如果当你的灵魂召唤你祷告你便只会哭泣，她就会边哭边抽打你，直到你笑出声来为止。

在你祈祷的时候，你站起来，升入空中，遇见正在这时祷告的人们，遇见不做祷告你就永远也可能见不上的人们。

praying at that very hour, and whom save in prayer you may not meet.

Therefore let your visit to that temple invisible be for naught but ecstasy and sweet communion.

For if you should enter the temple for no other purpose than asking you shall not receive.

And if you should enter into it to humble yourself you shall not be lifted:

Or even if you should enter into it to beg for the good of others you shall not be heard.

It is enough that you enter the temple invisible.


I cannot teach you how to pray in words.

God listens not to your words save when He Himself utters them through your lips.

And I cannot teach you the prayer of the seas and the forests and the mountains.

But you who are born of the mountains and the forests and the seas can find their prayer in your heart,

And if you but listen in the stillness of the night you shall hear them saying in silence, "Our God, who art our winged self,

所以，让你去那座隐秘的神殿造访，只为了狂迷和甜美的交流。

因为如果你进入了庙宇，没有别的目的，只是为了索求，你就不应该接受。

如果你进入这座庙宇，以使自己卑谦，那你便不会得到提升：

或者即使你进去，为他人求得好处，你也不会被倾听。

你只要进入那隐秘的神殿就够了。


我无法教你怎样用语言祷告。

神听的不是你的语言，除非"他自己"通过你的唇舌说出来。

我无法教你大海、森林、群山的祷告辞。

可是你们这些生于群山、森林、大海的人，在你心中便可以找到它们的祷文，

如果你只在夜的静谧中聆听，你应听见它们静默无声地说："我们的神啊，您是我们长有羽翼的自我，是您的意志在我们身上赋予了意志。

it is thy will in us that willeth.

It is thy desire in us that desireth.

It is thy urge in us that would turn our nights, which are thine, into days which are thine also.

We cannot ask thee for aught, for thou knowest our needs before they are born in us:

Thou art our need; and in giving us more of thyself thou givest us all."

是您的欲望在我们身上形成了欲望。

是您在我们体内的冲动，把我们的夜晚，原本也是您的夜晚，变成了同样属于您的白天。

我们不能向您索求任何东西，因为在我们的身上形成以前，您就早已洞察到我们的需要了：

您是我们的需要；把您自己给我们越多，您就给了我们一切。"

# Pleasure

Then a hermit, who visited the city once a year, came forth and said, Speak to us of Pleasure.

And he answered, saying:

Pleasure is a freedom song,

But it is not freedom.

It is the blossoming of your desires,

But it is not their fruit.

It is a depth calling unto a height,

But it is not the deep nor the high.

It is the caged taking wing,

But it is not space encompassed.

Ay, in very truth, pleasure is a freedom-song.

And I fain would have you sing it with fullness of heart; yet I would not have you lose your hearts in the singing.

# 快乐

然后，一位一年造访一次的隐士走上前说："跟我们讲讲快乐吧"。

他回答说：

快乐是一首自由之歌，

但它不是自由。

是你的种种欲望正在像花朵一样开放，

但不是它们的果实。

它是深度对高度的一种呼唤，

可它既不是深处也不是高处。

它是笼中之物找到了翅膀，

但它不是围起来的空间。

是啊，千真万确，快乐是一首自由之歌。

我很愿意你全心全意地唱一首；然而，你歌唱的时候，我不愿你们迷失了自己的心。

Some of your youth seek pleasure as if it were all, and they are judged and rebuked.

I would not judge nor rebuke them. I would have them seek.

For they shall find pleasure, but not her alone:

Seven are her sisters, and the least of them is more beautiful than pleasure.

Have you not heard of the man who was digging in the earth for roots and found a treasure?

And some of your elders remember pleasures with regret like wrongs committed in drunkenness.

But regret is the beclouding of the mind and not its chastisement.

They should remember their pleasures with gratitude, as they would the harvest of a summer.

Yet if it comforts them to regret, let them be comforted.


And there are among you those who are neither young to seek nor old to remember;

And in their fear of seeking and remembering they shun all pleasures, lest they neglect the spirit or offend against it.

你们当中一部分年轻人追求快乐，似乎那就是一切，于是他们受到了审判和斥责。

我不愿审判，也不愿斥责。我愿让他们去寻求。

因为他们应该找到快乐，但仅仅是快乐是不够的；

快乐有七个姊妹，其中最次的一个也比她本人漂亮。

你没有听说有人在地下挖根发现了宝藏吗？

你们中一些年长之人想起快乐，就带着遗憾，就像醉酒时犯下了错误。

但遗憾是心灵起了乌云，而不是对它的惩罚。

他们想起他们的快乐，就应该充满感激，就像他们收获一个夏季也会充满感激一样。

然而，如果遗憾让他们感到舒服，就让他们感到舒服吧。


你们当中有些人年轻时不追求，年老时也不回忆；

他们害怕追求，害怕回忆，逃避所有的快乐，以免忽视了精神，冒犯了它。

But even in their foregoing is their pleasure.

And thus they too find a treasure though they dig for roots with quivering hands.

But tell me, who is he that can offend the spirit?

Shall the nightingale offend the stillness of the night, or the firefly the stars?

And shall your flame or your smoke burden the wind?

Think you the spirit is a still pool which you can trouble with a staff?


Oftentimes in denying yourself pleasure you do but store the desire in the recesses of your being.

Who knows but that which seems omitted today, waits for tomorrow?

Even your body knows its heritage and its rightful need and will not be deceived.

And your body is the harp of your soul,

And it is yours to bring forth sweet music from it or confused sounds.


And now you ask in your heart, "How shall we distinguish

可即便在他们的放弃中，他们也有快乐。

于是他们也发现了一个宝藏，虽然他们挖根的时候手在颤抖。

可是告诉我，能冒犯精神的那位是谁？

是夜莺要冒犯夜的寂静，还是萤火虫要冒犯星星？

你的火焰或烟雾会成为风的负担吗？

莫非你认为精神是一潭静水你可以用一根棍子搅和吗？

很多时候你自己拒不享乐，直把欲望埋葬在你休眠的自我中。

谁知道今天看起来省掉的不是在等待明天呢？

即便你的身体，也知道自己的遗产和正当的需要，不会受到欺骗。

你的肉体是你灵魂的竖琴，

谁不知道，是那竖琴发出甜美的音乐，或是混淆不清的声响。

现在你扪心自问："快乐中好的和不好的，我们该如

that which is good in pleasure from that which is not good? "

Go to your fields and your gardens, and you shall learn that it is the pleasure of the bee to gather honey of the flower,

But it is also the pleasure of the flower to yield its honey to the bee.

For to the bee a flower is a fountain of life,

And to the flower a bee is a messenger of love,

And to both, bee and flower, the giving and the receiving of pleasure is a need and an ecstasy.


People of Orphalese, be in your pleasures like the flowers and the bees.

何区别？"

回到你的田地和花园，你会知道蜜蜂采花收蜜是它的快乐，

但是花儿把蜜糖交给蜜蜂也是快乐。

因为对于蜜蜂来说，花朵是生命的源泉，

对于花朵来说，蜜蜂是爱的信使，

对于蜜蜂和花朵双方，给予和接受快乐是一种需要，一种狂迷。



奥菲利斯的人民啦，跟花朵与蜜蜂一样享受快乐吧。

# Beauty

And a poet said, Speak to us of Beauty.

And he answered:

Where shall you seek beauty, and how shall you find her unless she herself be your way and your guide?

And how shall you speak of her except she be the weaver of your speech?

The aggrieved and the injured say, "Beauty is kind and gentle.

Like a young mother half-shy of her own glory she walks among us."

And the passionate say, "Nay, beauty is a thing of might and dread.

Like the tempest she shakes the earth beneath us and the sky above us."

# 美

一位诗人说："跟我们谈谈美吧。"

他回答说：

在你寻找美的地方，如果美自身不是你的道路和向导，你怎样才能找到她？

要是她不成为你话语的编织者，你怎么谈论她？

受了冤屈和伤害的人说："美既善良又温柔。

像一位年轻的母亲，对自己的荣耀带着几分羞涩，她在我们当中行走。"

激情满怀的人说："不，美是一件强力而令人恐怖的东西。

一如狂风暴雨，她上震苍穹，下撼大地。"

The tired and the weary say, "Beauty is of soft whisperings. She speaks in our spirit.

Her voice yields to our silences like a faint light that quivers in fear of the shadow."

But the restless say, "We have heard her shouting among the mountains,

And with her cries came the sound of hoofs, and the beating of wings and the roaring of lions."

At night the watchmen of the city say, "Beauty shall rise with the dawn from the east."

And at noontide the toilers and the wayfarers say, "we have seen her leaning over the earth from the windows of the sunset."

In winter say the snow-bound, "She shall come with the spring leaping upon the hills."

And in the summer heat the reapers say, "We have seen her dancing with the autumn leaves, and we saw a drift of snow in her hair."

困倦疲惫的人说："美是柔和的悄悄话。她在我们的精神里说话。

她的声音在我们的寂静中波动，像微弱的光因为害怕影子而震颤。"

烦躁不安的人说："我们听见她在崇山峻岭之间吼叫。

她的叫声引来了马蹄之声，飞鸟展翅之声，雄狮吼叫之声。"

夜晚，城里的守夜人说："美将伴随晨曦从东方升起。"

正午的劳苦人和赶路者说："我们从落日的窗户里看见她斜倚在大地上。"

冬天被雪所困的人说："她将和春天一起，从小山上蹦蹦跳跳地走下来。"

夏天酷热难当，收割庄稼的人说："我们看见她和秋叶一起舞蹈，在她的发梢里，我们看见一绺儿白雪。"

All these things have you said of beauty.

Yet in truth you spoke not of her but of needs unsatisfied,

And beauty is not a need but an ecstasy.

It is not a mouth thirsting nor an empty hand stretched forth,

But rather a heart enflamed and a soul enchanted.

It is not the image you would see nor the song you would hear,

But rather an image you see though you close your eyes and a song you hear though you shut your ears.

It is not the sap within the furrowed bark, nor a wing attached to a claw,

But rather a garden for ever in bloom and a flock of angels for ever in flight.


People of Orphalese, beauty is life when life unveils her holy face.

But you are life and you are the veil.

Beauty is eternity gazing at itself in a mirror.

But you are eternity and your are the mirror.

关于美，所有这些你们都说到了。

可事实上你们说的不是她，而是没有满足的需要。

美不是需要而是狂迷。

它不是焦渴的嘴唇，也不是伸出的空空的手，

而是一颗燃烧的心，一个着了迷的灵魂。

他不是你想看的形象，也不是你想听的歌声，

而是你闭着双眼也看得见的形象，你塞着耳朵也听得见的歌声。

它不是皱巴巴的树皮里的汁液，也不是附在爪子上的翅膀，

而是永远盛开鲜花的园林，一群永飞不止的天使。

奥菲利斯的人们啦！当生命揭开她神圣的面纱的时候，美就是生命。

可你既是生命，也是面纱。

美是在镜子里看着自己的永恒。

可你既是永恒也是镜子。

# Religion

And an old priest said, Speak to us of Religion.

And he said:

Have I spoken this day of aught else?

Is not religion all deeds and all reflection,

And that which is neither deed nor reflection, but a wonder and a surprise ever springing in the soul, even while the hands hew the stone or tend the loom?

Who can separate his faith from his actions, or his belief from his occupations?

Who can spread his hours before him, saying, "This for God and this for myself; This for my soul, and this other for my body? "

All your hours are wings that beat through space from self to self.

He who wears his morality but as his best garment were

# 宗教

一位老教士说："跟我们讲讲宗教吧。"

他回答说：

难道今天我讲的都是别的东西？

难道宗教不都是行为和反思吗？

难道它既不是行为也不是反思，而是双手还在掘石或织布的时候，从灵魂深处跳出的意外或惊奇？

谁能把信仰和行动、信念和职业分开呢？

谁能把时光摆在面前说："这是给神的，这是给我自己的；这是给我的灵魂的，这另外一部分是给我的肉体的？"

你所有的时刻分秒，都是从自己到自己穿越太空的翅膀。

有人穿上道德，作为他最好的衣服，倒不如光裸着身子。

better naked.

The wind and the sun will tear no holes in his skin.

And he who defines his conduct by ethics imprisons his song-bird in a cage.

The freest song comes not through bars and wires.

And he to whom worshipping is a window, to open but also to shut, has not yet visited the house of his soul whose windows are from dawn to dawn.


Your daily life is your temple and your religion.

Whenever you enter into it take with you your all.

Take the plough and the forge and the mallet and the lute,

The things you have fashioned in necessity or for delight.

For in revery you cannot rise above your achievements nor fall lower than your failures.

And take with you all men:

For in adoration you cannot fly higher than their hopes nor humble yourself lower than their despair.


And if you would know God be not therefore a solver of riddles.

风和太阳不会把他的皮肤撕出漏洞。

用伦理定义自己的行为之人把他会唱歌的鸟儿关进了笼子里。

最自由的歌不是从栏栅和铁网里来的。

对于他来说，膜拜是一扇窗，打开也关上，这种人却没有拜访过自己灵魂的房舍，那里的窗户从黎明开到第二天黎明。


你的日常生活是你的庙宇和你的宗教。

不论何时你进入，带上你的一切。

带上犁，带上炼铁炉，带上大斧头，带上诗琴，

带上那些你觉得需要或可让你高兴而铸成的东西，

因为在冥想之中，你不能升腾到高过自己的成就的地方，也不能跌落到低于你自己的失败的地方。

把所有的人都带上：

因为仰慕的时候，你不能飞得比他们的期望还高，也不能自贬自谦，低于他们的绝望。


如果你想认识神，那便不要好事揭开谜底。

Rather look about you and you shall see Him playing with your children.

And look into space; you shall see Him walking in the cloud, outstretching His arms in the lightning and descending in rain.

You shall see Him smiling in flowers, then rising and waving His hands in trees.

最好是看看周围，你会发现他在和你的孩子们一起玩耍。

看看太空；你会看见他在云彩间行走，把他的双手伸进闪电，在雨中下降。

你会看见他在花丛中微笑，然后站起身来，在树丛中挥动他的双手。

# Death

Then Almitra spoke, saying, We would ask now of Death.

And he said:

You would know the secret of death.

But how shall you find it unless you seek it in the heart of life?

The owl whose night-bound eyes are blind unto the day cannot unveil the mystery of light.

If you would indeed behold the spirit of death, open your heart wide unto the body of life.

For life and death are one, even as the river and the sea are one.

In the depth of your hopes and desires lies your silent knowledge of the beyond;

And like seeds dreaming beneath the snow your heart

# 死亡

　　然后阿尔米特拉说话了，她说："我们现在想问问死亡。"

　　他说：

　　你会知道死亡的秘密的。

　　可是，如果你不在生命的心中寻找，你怎么能找到它？

　　猫头鹰的夜眼看不见白天，也就无法揭开光神秘的面纱。

　　如果你真的想要看见死亡的精魂，敞开胸怀拥抱生命的肉体吧。

　　因为生和死是同一的，正如江河和大海是同一的一样。


　　在你希望和欲望的深处躺着关于彼岸默默的知识；

　　像种子在冬雪下面做梦一样，你的心梦见春天。

dreams of spring.

Trust the dreams, for in them is hidden the gate to eternity.

Your fear of death is but the trembling of the shepherd when he stands before the king whose hand is to be laid upon him in honour.

Is the shepherd not joyful beneath his trembling, that he shall wear the mark of the king?

Yet is he not more mindful of his trembling?

For what is it to die but to stand naked in the wind and to melt into the sun?

And what is to cease breathing, but to free the breath from its restless tides, that it may rise and expand and seek God unencumbered?

Only when you drink from the river of silence shall you indeed sing.

And when you have reached the mountain top, then you shall begin to climb.

And when the earth shall claim your limbs, then shall you truly dance.

相信梦吧，因为它们当中藏着通向永恒的大门。

你惧怕死亡，只不过是当牧羊人站在国王面前，国王的手很荣幸地放在他的身上，他就发抖。

在这样的颤抖之下，牧羊人要佩戴国王的标记，他不觉得高兴么？

可是他不还是更加在乎他的颤抖么？

因为死亡不就是赤裸裸地站在风中，融化到太阳里吗？

停止呼吸是什么？它只不过是让气息从无休无止的浪潮中解脱出来，它可以升起、扩展、无牵无挂地追寻神？

当且仅当你啜饮寂静之河的时候，你才能真正地歌唱。

当你达到山巅，那时你才可能开始攀登。

当大地要求你献出身体的时候，你才会真正开始舞蹈。

# The Farewell

And now it was evening.

And Almitra the seeress said, Blessed be this day and this place and your spirit that has spoken.

And he answered, Was it I who spoke? Was I not also a listener?

Then he descended the steps of the Temple and all the people followed him. And he reached his ship and stood upon the deck.

And facing the people again, he raised his voice and said:

People of Orphalese, the wind bids me leave you. Less hasty am I than the wind, yet I must go.

We wanderers, ever seeking the lonelier way, begin no day where we have ended another day; and no sunrise finds us where sunset left us.

Even while the earth sleeps we travel.

# 告别辞

现在到了黄昏时分。

阿尔米特拉女先知说:"今天,这个地方,还有你说话的心灵都得到了祝福。"

他回答说,是我在说话么?我不也是一个聆听者么?

然后他从寺庙的台阶拾级而下,所有的人都追随着他。他走到航船跟前,上了船,站在甲板上。

他再一次面对人们,提高声音说:

奥菲利斯的人民啊,风要我离开你们。

我没有风那么急,可我不得不走。

我们这些漂泊者,总是在寻找更为孤寂的路,从不在结束一天的地方开始另一天,日出也不在日落离开我们的地方找到我们。

甚至大地沉睡的时候我们还在旅行!

We are the seeds of the tenacious plant, and it is in our ripeness and our fullness of heart that we are given to the wind and are scattered.

Brief were my days among you, and briefer still the words I have spoken.

But should my voice fade in your ears, and my love vanish in your memory, then I will come again,

And with a richer heart and lips more yielding to the spirit will I speak.

Yea, I shall return with the tide,

And though death may hide me, and the greater silence enfold me, yet again will I seek your understanding.

And not in vain will I seek.

If aught I have said is truth, that truth shall reveal itself in a clearer voice, and in words more kin to your thoughts.

I go with the wind, people of Orphalese, but not down into emptiness;

And if this day is not a fulfillment of your needs and my love, then let it be a promise till another day.

我们是顽强的植物的种子，是在我们的成熟和心的完善中，把我们交给了风，再把我们播撒。


我在你们当中的日子很短，我说的话就更短。

可要是我的声音从你们的耳朵里消失，我的爱从你们的记忆中减退，我就再回到你们身边，

我回来的时候，我要带着一颗更为富足的心，更为切合我内心的双唇，来给你们说话。

是啊，潮已涨起，我得回去了，

虽然死亡会把我藏起来，更大的沉寂包裹着我，可我仍然要寻求你们的理解。

我的寻求不会白费。

如果我说的有一点儿是真理，这个真理就会用更清晰的声音显示自己，用与你们的思想更亲近的词句来揭示。


奥菲利斯的人民，我随风去了，但不是沉入虚空；

如果今天没有满足你们的需要，没有充分实施我的爱，就让它成为一个诺言留待来日吧。

Man's needs change, but not his Love, nor his desire that his love should satisfy his needs.

Know therefore, that from the greater silence I shall return.

The mist that drifts away at dawn, leaving but dew in the fields, shall rise and gather into a cloud and then fall down in rain.

And not unlike the mist have I been.

In the stillness of the night I have walked in your streets, and my spirit has entered your houses,

And your heart-beats were in my heart, and your breath was upon my face, and I knew you all.

Ay, I knew your joy and your pain, and in your sleep your dreams were my dreams.

And oftentimes I was among you a lake among the mountains.

I mirrored the summits in you and the bending slopes, and even the passing flocks of your thoughts and your desires.

And to my silence came the laughter of your children in streams, and the longing of your youths in rivers.

And when they reached my depth the streams and the rivers ceased not yet to sing.

人的需要在变，但是他的爱不会变，他那满足他种种需要的欲望也不会变。

所以要知道，我要从更深的静默中回来。

清晨游弋的迷雾，只把露珠留在田野里，就要升起聚成云朵，以雨的形式降下。

一直以来，我跟这迷雾并无两样。

在夜晚的寂静里，我在你们的街上行走，我的精神进入了你们的房舍，

你们的心跳在我的心中，你们的呼吸在我的脸上，你们的一切我都知道。

是的，我知道你们的欢乐和痛苦，你们的睡梦也就是我的睡梦。

我经常在你们当中就像湖泊在群山之中。

你们的山峰从我的镜子中映照出来，还有你们起伏不平的山坡，甚至你们一群群地经过的思想和欲望。

冲着我的沉默传来了溪涧里你们的孩子们的笑声，传来了江河里你们年轻人的渴望。

当它们到达我的深处，溪流、江河仍不停止歌唱。

But sweeter still than laughter and greater than longing came to me.

It was boundless in you;

The vast man in whom you are all but cells and sinews;

He in whose chant all your singing is but a soundless throbbing.

It is in the vast man that you are vast,

And in beholding him that I beheld you and loved you.

For what distances can love reach that are not in that vast sphere?

What visions, what expectations and what presumptions can outsoar that flight?

Like a giant oak tree covered with apple blossoms is the vast man in you.

His might binds you to the earth, his fragrance lifts you into space, and in his durability you are deathless.


You have been told that, even like a chain, you are as weak as your weakest link.

This is but half the truth. You are also as strong as your strongest link.

但比笑声更为甜美的，比渴望更为伟大的到我这里来了。

它是你们身上的无限；

在一个巨人身上，你们只不过是细胞和筋肌；

在他的歌声里，你们所有的歌唱只不过是没有声响的悸动而已。

是在巨人的身上你们才巨大起来，

因为看见了他，我才看见了你们，热爱你们。

爱能到达什么样的距离才不在那无垠的范围之内？

什么样的视野，什么样的期待，什么样的推测可以超越那样的飞翔？

像一棵巨大的橡树，满缀着苹果花，那是巨人在你们身体内。

他的力量把你缚在大地上，他的香气把你升入太空，在他的永恒里你是永生不朽的。


有人告诉你说，正如一根链条，你是其中最弱的一环。

这只说对了一半：你很结实，也是其中最结实的一环。

To measure you by your smallest deed is to reckon the power of ocean by the frailty of its foam.

To judge you by your failures is to cast blame upon the seasons for their inconsistency.


Ay, you are like an ocean,

And though heavy-grounded ships await the tide upon your shores, yet, even like an ocean, you cannot hasten your tides.

And like the seasons you are also,

And though in your winter you deny your spring,

Yet spring, reposing within you, smiles in her drowsiness and is not offended.

Think not I say these things in order that you may say the one to the other, "He praised us well. He saw but the good in us."

I only speak to you in words of that which you yourselves know in thought.

And what is word knowledge but a shadow of wordless knowledge?

Your thoughts and my words are waves from a sealed

用你的最小的行为去衡量你，是用大海泡沫的脆弱去估价整个大海的力量。

用你的失败去判断你，那是责备四季，说它们不够专一。


啊，你像大海，

虽然负载沉重的航船等待你的沙滩涨起潮汐，即使像大海一样，你也不能匆忙驱赶你的潮汐。

你也像四季，

虽是在寒冬，你也拒不承认春天，

可是春天在你体内休息，在困倦中微笑，没有被惹恼不快。

不要以为我说这些以便你们可以互相说："他好生表扬了我们，他在我们身上只看到了好的那一面。"

我只用你们自己在思想中所认识的那种语言跟你们说话。

有文字的知识若不是无文字的知识的影子，那种知识又是什么？

你们的思想和我的语言是尘封的记忆中的波涛，保留着我们昨天的记录，

memory that keeps records of our yesterdays,

And of the ancient days when the earth knew not us nor herself,

And of nights when earth was upwrought with confusion.


Wise men have come to you to give you of their wisdom. I came to take of your wisdom:

And behold I have found that which is greater than wisdom.

It is a flame spirit in you ever gathering more of itself,

While you, heedless of its expansion, bewail the withering of your days.

It is life in quest of life in bodies that fear the grave.


There are no graves here.

These mountains and plains are a cradle and a stepping-stone.

Whenever you pass by the field where you have laid your ancestors look well thereupon, and you shall see yourselves and your children dancing hand in hand.

Verily you often make merry without knowing.

保留了我们遥远的白昼的记录，那时大地不认识我们，也不认识她自己，

还保留了夜晚的记录，那时大地还是铸造中的一片混沌。


哲人到你们跟前来，把他们的智慧交给你们，我来从你们当中获取智慧：

看啊，我发现了比智慧更伟大的东西。

那是你们身上精神的火焰把自己越聚越多；

而你们没有注意到它在扩展，哀叹日子在枯萎。

那是生命在惧怕坟墓的肉体里追求生命。


这里没有坟墓。

这些群山和平原只是一个摇篮，一块铺路石。

每当你走过这片你曾安葬了你们的祖先的田野，你仔细看看，你会看见自己和孩子们手牵着手在上面跳舞。

事实上，你们常常寻欢作乐，自己却浑然不知。

Others have come to you to whom for golden promises made unto your faith you have given but riches and power and glory.

Less than a promise have I given, and yet more generous have you been to me.

You have given me deeper thirsting after life.

Surely there is no greater gift to a man than that which turns all his aims into parching lips and all life into a fountain.

And in this lies my honour and my reward, —

That whenever I come to the fountain to drink I find the living water itself thirsty;

And it drinks me while I drink it.


Some of you have deemed me proud and over-shy to receive gifts.

Too proud indeed am I to receive wages, but not gifts.

And though I have eaten berries among the hill when you would have had me sit at your board,

And slept in the portico of the temple where you would gladly have sheltered me,

Yet was it not your loving mindfulness of my days and my

其他的人到你们这里来，为了他给你们的信仰许下金光闪闪的诺言，你们给他们的不过是财富、权力和荣耀。

我给的远不如一个承诺，可是你们对我慷慨得多。

你们给了我对生命更加深厚的渴望。

对于一个人来说，能把自己全部的目标变成焦渴的嘴唇，把整个生命变成甘泉，毫无疑问，没有比这更了不起的礼物了。

这当中有我的荣誉和收获，

不论何时我来到泉边饮水，我发现这活生生的泉水自己也是焦渴的；

我啜饮它的时候，它也在啜饮我。


你们当中有些人认为我接受礼物时高傲，或过于害臊。

我的确很高傲，不愿接受酬劳，可礼物不一样。

虽然我在山间吃野果，而不坐在你们家的餐桌旁，

你们愿意高高兴兴地让我住你们家里，我却睡在寺庙里的门廊中，

难道不是因为你们白天黑夜挂念我，爱护我，我的

nights that made food sweet to my mouth and girdled my sleep with visions?

For this I bless you most:

You give much and know not that you give at all.

Verily the kindness that gazes upon itself in a mirror turns to stone,

And a good deed that calls itself by tender names becomes the parent to a curse.

And some of you have called me aloof, and drunk with my own aloneness,

And you have said, "He holds council with the trees of the forest, but not with men.

He sits alone on hill-tops and looks down upon our city."

True it is that I have climbed the hills and walked in remote places.

How could I have seen you save from a great height or a great distance?

How can one be indeed near unless he be far?

食物才甘甜可口，我的梦里才有美景环绕吗？


因此，我最诚挚地祝福你们：

你们给的太多甚至不知道你们在给予。

事实上，在镜子里紧盯着自己的那种善良变成了顽石，

善举用美名称呼自己变成了诅咒的父母。


你们有些人说我避世，醉心于自己的孤独，

你们说："他以森林树木为伴，不和人打堆。

他独自坐在山顶上，俯视我们的城市。"

我翻山越岭走在荒无人烟的地方，那是真的。

不从很高或很远的地方我怎么能够看得见你们？

一个人不离远一点儿他怎么才可以真正接近呢？

And others among you called unto me, not in words, and they said,

"Stranger, stranger, lover of unreachable heights, why dwell you among the summits where eagles build their nests?

Why seek you the unattainable?

What storms would you trap in your net,

And what vaporous birds do you hunt in the sky?

Come and be one of us.

Descend and appease your hunger with our bread and quench your thirst with our wine."

In the solitude of their souls they said these things;

But were their solitude deeper they would have known that I sought but the secret of your joy and your pain,

And I hunted only your larger selves that walk the sky.


But the hunter was also the hunted;

For many of my arrows left my bow only to seek my own breast.

And the flier was also the creeper;

For when my wings were spread in the sun their shadow upon the earth was a turtle.

你们当中的其他人呼唤我，不是用语言，他们说：

"陌生人，陌生人，喜欢高不可攀的地方的人，为什么住在老鹰筑巢的山峰之间啊？

为什么追寻得不到的东西？

在你的网里你要收罗什么样的暴风雨，

你要狩猎天上什么样的空幻的鸟儿？

来吧，来加入我们吧。

下来吃面包止饿，喝葡萄酒解渴吧。"

他们的灵魂孤寂便说了这些话；

可是假如他们的孤寂再深些，他们便应该知道，我寻找的，只不过是你们欢乐和痛苦的秘密，

我追猎的只是在天上行走的你们更大的自我。



可是猎人也被别人捕猎；

因为很多离开我的弓的箭要寻找的，是我自己的胸膛。

飞行者也是爬行者；

因为当我的羽翼在太阳底下展开，它在大地上的影子只是一只乌龟。

And I the believer was also the doubter;

For often have I put my finger in my own wound that I might have the greater belief in you and the greater knowledge of you.

And it is with this belief and this knowledge that I say,

You are not enclosed within your bodies, nor confined to houses or fields.

That which is you dwells above the mountain and roves with the wind.

It is not a thing that crawls into the sun for warmth or digs holes into darkness for safety,

But a thing free, a spirit that envelops the earth and moves in the ether.

If these be vague words, then seek not to clear them.

Vague and nebulous is the beginning of all things, but not their end,

And I fain would have you remember me as a beginning.

Life, and all that lives, is conceived in the mist and not in the crystal.

And who knows but a crystal is mist in decay?

还有，我这个信徒也是怀疑者；

因为我经常把手指伸进自己的伤口，这样我便可能对你们有更大的信任，才可能更多地认识你们。

正是因为这个信任和认识，我说，

你并不是包裹在自己的身体之中的，也没有被关在房舍中、田野里。

是你们的那些东西住在群山之上，和风一起翱翔。

它不是一个爬进太阳找寻温暖，打洞钻进黑暗寻求安稳的动物，

而是一件自由之物，一种精神，包卷着大地，在天宇之中运行。

如果这些话晦涩难懂的话，不要把它们搞清楚。

万物伊始便是晦涩朦胧，不明形体的，但这不是它们的结局，

我宁愿你们把我当成开始来记住我，

生命，所有活着的东西，都是在迷雾中而不是水晶中孕育出来的。

可谁又知道水晶只不过是腐朽中的迷雾？

This would I have you remember in remembering me:

That which seems most feeble and bewildered in you is the strongest and most determined.

Is it not your breath that has erected and hardened the structure of your bones?

And is it not a dream which none of you remember having dreamt that building your city and fashioned all there is in it?

Could you but see the tides of that breath you would cease to see all else,

And if you could hear the whispering of the dream you would hear no other sound.

But you do not see, nor do you hear, and it is well.

The veil that clouds your eyes shall be lifted by the hands that wove it,

And the clay that fills your ears shall be pierced by those fingers that kneaded it.

And you shall see

And you shall hear.

我愿你们记住我时记住这些：

在你们身上表面看来最柔弱、最迷茫的其实最结实、最坚定。

难道不是你们的气息竖起并稳固了你的骨骼吗？

难道不是梦，一个你们谁也不记得了的梦，建成了你们的城池，造出了那里的一切？


要是你们能看见那气息的浪潮，你们便会停止看别的一切，

假如你们能听见梦的呢喃，你们就不想听见所有其他的声音。


可是你们看不见也听不见，这很好。

遮住你们双眼的面纱应该由织纱的手来揭开，

堵塞你们耳朵的黏土应该由制作黏土的手指来通开。

你会看得见

你会听得见。

Yet you shall not deplore having known blindness, nor regret having been deaf.

For in that day you shall know the hidden purposes in all things,

And you shall bless darkness as you would bless light.


After saying these things he looked about him, and he saw the pilot of his ship standing by the helm and gazing now at the full sails and now at the distance.


And he said:

Patient, over-patient, is the captain of my ship.

The wind blows, and restless are the sails;

Even the rudder begs direction;

Yet quietly my captain awaits my silence.

And these my mariners, who have heard the choir of the greater sea, they too have heard me patiently.

Now they shall wait no longer.

I am ready.

The stream has reached the sea, and once more the great mother holds her son against her breast.

可是你不应后悔认识了盲目，也不应后悔曾经失聪。

因为到那一天你会知道万物隐秘的意图，

你会像祝福光明那样祝福黑暗。


说完这些话他环顾四周，他看见航船的舵手站在舵轮旁，一会儿看着涨满的风帆，一会儿凝视着远方。


然后他说：

耐心，太有耐心了，我那船长。

风在劲吹，焦急烦躁的是那风帆；

甚至舵盘都在乞求方向；

尽管如此，船长在静静地等候我的沉默。

我的这些水手，已经听见大海远处的合唱，他们也耐心地听着我。

现在他们不用再等下去了。

我已准备就绪。

溪流已到达大海，伟大的母亲再一次把儿子怀抱在胸前。

Fare you well, people of Orphalese.

This day has ended.

It is closing upon us even as the water-lily upon its own tomorrow.

What was given us here we shall keep,

And if it suffices not, then again must we come together and together stretch our hands unto the giver.

Forget not that I shall come back to you.

A little while, and my longing shall gather dust and foam for another body.

A little while, a moment of rest upon the wind, and another woman shall bear me.


Farewell to you and the youth I have spent with you.

It was but yesterday we met in a dream.

You have sung to me in my aloneness, and I of your longings have built a tower in the sky.

But now our sleep has fled and our dream is over, and it is no longer dawn.

别了，奥菲利斯的人民。

这一天结束了。

它正向我们关闭，正如向着它自己的明天合上的睡莲。

在这里给我们的我们会保留起来，

如果还不够，我们就再一次聚在一起，一起向给予者伸出我们的双手。

不要忘了，我要回到你们身边的。

过一会儿，我的渴望会把尘埃和泡沫收集起来，去制作另一个肉体。

过一会儿，在风上休息片刻，另一个女人会把我生出来。


再见了，你们还有和我一起度过的青春。

我们一起在梦里相会，那只不过是昨天。

在我孤独的时候你们为我歌唱，为你们的渴望我在空中建立了一座高楼。

可是现在我们睡意已去，梦已醒，天已不是拂晓。

The noontide is upon us and our half waking has turned to fuller day, and we must part.

If in the twilight of memory we should meet once more, we shall speak again together and you shall sing to me a deeper song.

And if our hands should meet in another dream, we shall build another tower in the sky.


So saying he made a signal to the seamen, and straightaway they weighed anchor and cast the ship loose from its moorings, and they moved eastward.

And a cry came from the people as from a single heart, and it rose the dusk and was carried out over the sea like a great trumpeting.

Only Almitra was silent, gazing after the ship until it had vanished into the mist.

And when all the people were dispersed she still stood alone upon the sea-wall, remembering in her heart his saying,


"A little while, a moment of rest upon the wind, and another woman shall bear me."

正午压在我们身上，我们半睡半醒，到了中天，我们必须分手了。

如果记忆的黄昏里我们必须重逢，我们将在一起说话，你们给我唱一首更深沉的歌。

如果我们的手，要在另一个梦里相遇，我们就在空中建起另一座高楼。


这样说着，他朝水手们做了一个手势，他们直直地起锚，把船从系泊处松开，朝东驶去。

一声呼喊从人群中升起，仿佛从单单的一颗心里升起，它升入黄昏，传向远处的大海上空，像号角的巨响。

只有阿尔米特拉一声不吭，一直凝视着远去的航船，直到它在迷雾里消失。

当所有的人都渐渐散去，她独自站在海堤上，心中想起他说过的一句话：



"过一会儿，在风上休息片刻，另一个女人会把我生出来。"

# 附录一　纪伯伦小传

纪伯伦·哈利勒·纪伯伦于 1883 年 1 月 6 日出生于黎巴嫩北部的小山村贝什里。按照传统习俗，他的名字使用了他祖父的名字，因而全名称作 "纪伯伦·哈利勒·纪伯伦"。在英语里，一般简称为 "哈利勒·纪伯伦"。按照英语的读音，应译为 "俞伯朗"（[ʒʊ'bra:n xa'li:l ʒʊ'bra:n]），现已约定俗成为 "纪伯伦"，并以此流传于世。

他十二岁的时候，举家移民至美国，因此成了黎巴嫩裔美国人，以作家、诗人和画家的身份流传后世。除了这些身份，虽然他自己拒不接受，却也被认为是一名哲学家。纪伯伦最有名的作品，是他 1923 年在美国出版的《先知》。这部作品，一出版就声名鹊起，畅销天下，使得一时洛阳纸贵。据 2008 年 1 月 7 日《纽约时报》一篇文章称，在畅销作家中，纪伯伦名列世界第三，居莎士比亚和老子之后。这部诗集如此受欢迎，竟然被译成了一百多种文字，受欢迎程度之高，简直令人拍案叫绝。自1923年初版，到2004年7月，仅美国版就历经140印，行销愈900万册。

纪伯伦的母亲以做裁缝女工为生，送儿子去波士顿上学。很快，他就小荷尖尖，初露头角，为摄影家兼出版商的弗雷德·霍兰德·戴伊所器重。纪伯伦十五岁的时候，被送回了他出生的祖国，去贝鲁特的德·拉·萨热斯学院上学。1902年回到波士顿，不幸的是，他的妹妹、兄弟和母亲都先后离世。靠着他姐姐的一点点裁缝店的收入，他度过了一些时日。

1904年，他的绘画首次在戴的画室展出，次年他的第一本用阿拉伯语写成的书在纽约出版。在另一位赞助人玛丽·哈斯克尔（Mary Haskell）的资助下，他去巴黎学习了三年绘画。在此期间，他结交了叙利亚的一些社会活动家，推动当时的叛乱。他的一些著作对此进行了描述，表达了自己的心声，酿成了后来奥托曼当局对他的驱逐。1911年，纪伯伦在纽约定居下来，出版了他的第一部英语创作《疯人》（*The Madman*），1918年由为他出版系列诗集与作品的艾尔弗雷德·A.诺普夫出版社出版。他的绘画分别于1914年和1917年在蒙特罗斯艺术馆（Montross Gallery）和诺德勒出版社（M. Knoedler & Co.）展出。

1920年他和其他马嘉瑞诗人一道，恢复成立了笔会。

到他 48 岁死于肝硬化和肺结核，他已经横跨大西洋的两岸名扬四海了。散文诗集《先知》已经被译成了德语和法语。他的遗体被运回到他的故乡，在那里安葬。

正如苏海勒·巴莎鲁伊（Suheil Bushrui）与乔·詹金斯（Joe Jenkins）所说，纪伯伦的一生已经处于"尼采式的反叛，布莱克式的泛神论以及苏菲式的神秘主义"之间了。

纪伯伦的作品里描述了数不胜数的艺术话题，探索了各式各样的文学样式。有人把他称作是二十世纪前半叶唯一对阿拉伯诗歌与文学影响最大的人；同时，他也被当成黎巴嫩的文坛英雄来加以膜拜。同样，纪伯伦大多数的绘画表现了他自己独特的眼光，把精神的象征与神话的象征水乳交融地融合在一起。批评家发现，他的身上承接了比其他任何一个现代艺术家都要多的达·芬奇传统，他汗牛充栋的创作被描述为所有民族所有人的艺术遗产。

# 附录二　纪伯伦大事年表

1883年1月6日　出生于黎巴嫩北部省的小山村贝什里。

1888年　就读于以赛亚修道院小学。

1895年　到达美国波士顿。

1895年9月　进入奥利佛附近的移民学校奎西中学学习，受到弗劳伦斯·皮尔斯的注意，被"儿童资助社团"的社会工作者杰西·弗莱蒙·比尔介绍给波士顿先锋派艺术的支持者、摄影艺术家、出版商弗雷德·霍兰德·戴伊。

1898年9月至1902年4月　返回黎巴嫩的贝鲁特学习阿拉伯语言文化。

1904年5月　在波士顿画廊举行首次个人画展，《灵魂皈依上帝》与《痛苦的喷泉》等画吸引了马尔莱布鲁街女子小学校长玛丽·伊莉莎白·哈斯克尔。

1905年　出版《音乐短章》。

1906年　出版短篇小说集《草原新娘》。

1907 年　发表短篇小说集《叛逆的灵魂》。

1908 年 7 月 1 日　前往巴黎学习绘画艺术，居住在巴黎先锋派艺术家聚居地蒙马特高地。

1910 年 10 月　回到波士顿，与玛丽成为一生的恋人和挚友。

1911 年冬天　阿拉伯语小说代表作《折断的翅膀》出版，被誉为"阿拉伯文学新运动的开端"。

1912 年　创作绘画《三个女人》；6 月 16 日，在纽约叙利亚妇女俱乐部发表演讲；同年，开始创作《暴风集》。

1913 年（约）4 月 16 日　《艺术》杂志主编纳西布·阿里德汇集了《泪与笑》全集出版。

1914 年 2 月　在蒙特鲁斯大厅举行个人画展，展出 75 幅作品。

1915 年　任叙利亚难民救济委员会会长。

1916 年　纪伯伦与文学家米哈依勒·努埃曼结交。

1920 年 4 月　"笔会"正式成立，当选为笔会会长；5 月 20 日前夕，在科学技术学会发表演讲。8 月中旬，出版《先驱者》。

1923 年 5 月 8 日　尤素福·托玛·布斯塔尼在埃及为纪伯伦出版《珍趣篇》。6 月 16 日重印《珍趣篇》。9 月 3 日、17 日中国《文学周刊》杂志分别发表茅盾从《先驱者》

中选译的五篇散文诗:《批评家》《张雪白的纸说》《价值》《别的海》《圣的愚者》;同年,在纽约克诺夫出版社出版《先知》。

1924年　穆罕默德·托基丁搜集其文章在埃及出版文论集《在文学世界》。其后,陆续为各界名流画像,包括威廉·萨默塞特·毛姆等人,绘画作品相继在各地展出。

1926年　正式发表《沙与沫》;应邀出任纽约《新东方》(*The New Orient*)杂志的编委。

1928年　完成《先知园》,开始写《流浪者》《大地诸神》;同年夏天,《人之子耶稣》完稿。

1929年　健康状况恶化,并将大部分时间用于绘画、著述、校订等方面;同年,开始构思论威廉·莎士比亚、米开朗基罗·博那罗蒂、巴鲁赫·斯宾诺莎和路德维希·凡·贝多芬的专著。

1931年4月10日　在美国纽约格林威治村圣芳心医院去世,终年48岁;8月21日,灵柩运回黎巴嫩,首都贝鲁特举行迎灵仪式;8月22日,送葬行列把遗体送回故乡,葬于贝什里圣徒谢尔基斯修道院。

# 附录三　纪伯伦著作目录

带★者为英文原创。

## 一、文学作品（Books）

1905 年　散文《音乐短章》（*A Profile of the Art of Music*）

1906 年　短篇小说《草原新娘》（*Nymphs of the Valley*）

1908 年　短篇小说《叛逆的灵魂》（*Spirits Rebellious*）

1912 年　长篇小说《折断的翅膀》（*Broken Wings*）

1914 年　散文诗集《泪与笑》（*A Tear and A Smile*，又译 *Tears and Laughter*, 1947）

1918 年　散文集《疯人》（*The Madman*）★

1918 年　诗集《行列圣歌》（*The Processions*）

1920 年　散文诗集《先驱者》（*The Forerunner*）★

1920 年　散文诗集《暴风雨》（*The Tempests*，又译 *The Storm*, 1994）

1923 年　散文诗集《先知》（*The Prophet*）★

1923 年　诗集《珍闻与趣谈》（*The New and the Marvelous*）

1926 年　散文诗集《沙与沫》( *Sand and Foam* ) ★

1927 年　诗集《与灵魂私语》( *Spiritual Sayings* )

1928 年　散文诗集《人子耶稣》( *Jesus, the Son of Man* ) ★

1931 年　诗剧《大地诸神》( *The Earth Gods* ) ★

1932 年　散文诗集《流浪者》( *The Wanderer* ) ★

1933 年　散文诗集《先知园》( *The Garden of the Prophet* ) ★

1933 年　诗剧《拉撒路和他的情人》( *Lazarus and his Beloved* ) ★

1934 年　《散文诗集》( *Prose Poems* )

1947 年　诗集《心的秘密》( *Secrets of the Heart* )

1959 年　书信集《自画像》( *A Self-Portrait* )

1960 年　诗集《沉思集》( *Thoughts and Meditations* )

1963 年　诗集《大师之音》( *Voice of the Master* )

1965 年　诗集《灵魂之镜》( *Mirrors of the Soul* )

1972 年　戏剧《昼夜之间》( *Between Night & Morn* )

1972 年　情书集《爱你如诗美丽》( *Beloved Prophet, The Love Letters of Khalil Gibran and Mary Haskell, and Her Private Journal* )

1993 年　戏剧《没有看见的人》( *The Man Unseen* )

1993 年　戏剧《染色之脸》( *The Colored Faces* )

1993 年　戏剧《革命的开端》( *The Beginning of the*

*Revolution*）

　　1993 年　戏剧《国王与牧羊人》（*The King and the Shepherd*）

　　1994 年　诗集《被爱者》（*The Beloved : Reflections on the Path of the Heart*）

　　1994 年　诗集《视野》（*The Vision*）

　　1995 年　诗集《先知眼》（*The Eye of the Prophet*）

　　年代不详　书信集《蓝色火焰》（*Blue Flame: The Love Letters of Kahlil Gibran to May Ziadah*）


## 二、绘画作品（Visual Art）

　　1910 年　《女人的不同时代》（*The Ages of Women*）现藏墨西哥城索马亚艺术博物馆（Museo Soumaya）

　　1911 年　《自画像与缪斯》（*Self-Portrait and Muse*）现藏墨西哥城索马亚艺术博物馆（Museo Soumaya）

　　1911 年　无题（《玫瑰袖子》）Untitled（*Rose Sleeves*）现藏萨凡纳特尔费尔博物馆（Telfair Museums）

　　1916 年　《走向无限》（*Towards the Infinite*，又被称为《母亲》）（Kamila Gibran，卡米拉，纪伯伦母亲的像）现藏纽约大都会博物馆（Metropolitan Museum of Arts）

　　1918 年　《三个女人》（*The Three Are One*）现藏萨凡纳特尔费尔博物馆（Telfair Museums）

1919 年 《二十幅画》（*Twenty Drawings*），画集。由阿尔弗雷德·D·诺普夫出版社（Alfred D. Knopf）出版，含《大我》(*Greater Self*)、《盲人》(*The Blind*)等。

1920 年 《奴隶》(*The Slave*)现藏哈佛艺术博物馆（Harvard Art Museums）

1923 年 《〈人子耶稣〉题画》(A sketch for *Jesus the Son of Man*, 1928) 现藏萨凡纳特尔费尔博物馆（Telfair Museums）

年代不详 《站立人与孩子》(*Standing Figure and Child*)现藏巴吉尔艺术基金会博物馆（Barjeel Art Foundation）

### 三、改编作品（Adaptations）

1962 年 《折断的翅膀》(*The Broken Wings*)

2014 年 《哈利勒·纪伯伦的先知》(*Kahlil Gibran's The Prophet*)

### 四、再创作（Inspirations）

1985 年 美国同名摇滚乐队"密斯特先生"（Mr Mister）歌曲《折断的翅膀》("Broken Wings")

1995 年 美国"疯狂季节"（Mad Season）摇滚乐队歌曲《欺骗的河流》("River of Deceit")

## 五、残篇

三部英语戏剧未完稿,未付梓。分别是:

(1)《报死女鬼》(*The Banshee*);

(2)《最后一次涂油礼》(*The Last Unction*);

(3)《驼背隐身人》(*The Hunchback or the Man Unseen*).

# 诗行不缺真本，《先知》又添新译

## ——读罗译纪伯伦诗集记事

### 朱法荣

一

人们常说，诗画同源，诗传意，画见形，是姊妹艺术。钱钟书先生则说，诗与画各有各的批评标准，可以用吴道子的画风来作诗，但且不可用杜甫的诗风来作画。对书画兼善的王维，钱先生称赞其雪里芭蕉禅味隽永，可坐南宗画（也即中国画）第一把交椅，"但是旧诗传统里排起座位来，首席是数不着他的。中唐以来，众望所归的最大诗人一直是杜甫。借用意大利人的说法，王维和杜甫相比，只能算是'小的大诗人'"①。然则，我们还是禁不住纳罕那些书画兼通之士，总觉得他们的诗更有色彩，画更有深意。

更让人不大想得到的是，现当代许多画家兼诗人还

---

① 钱钟书:《中国诗与中国画》(《比较文学研究资料》, 北京师范大学中文系比较文学研究组选编。北京: 北京师范大学出版社, 1986 年)。

都喜欢写散文诗。这可能与艺术的朴素化和就简化有关。从前，莎士比亚用无韵诗写戏剧，弥尔顿也用它写史诗，明显有一种从韵文向白话进化的过程和倾向。当然，莎士比亚和但丁用白话、俗语，不用韵，可能是在跟古希腊人的时髦。不过，散文诗（prose poem）之作为一种文学样式被文学行业接受并成为一种主流形式，源于法国诗人波德莱尔1869年发表的诗集名字《小散文诗》，也就是后来的《巴黎的忧郁》。在诗集献词中，波德莱尔介绍了自己写散文诗的目的和技巧："我们当中，谁没有在怀着雄心壮志的日子里，梦想过创造奇迹，写出诗的散文，没有节律，没有脚韵，但富于音乐性，而且亦刚亦柔，足以适应心灵抒情的冲动、幻想的波动和意识的跳跃？[①]"这种散文诗，是一种独特的艺术结构，可以抒情，可以叙事，但应该出于纯粹的诗意目的，必须简短、浓缩、发光，甚至令人震惊。仿佛一条蜿蜒的蛇，每一篇都交替地互为首尾，每一段都可以独立存在，读者可以随意中断，但是又可以毫无困难地重新衔接。之所以称为散文诗，而不是散文，就在于它有散文的形式，但其思想、结构、题材、情感和用词都遵循诗的规律，具有诗的品格，

---

① 〔法〕波德莱尔：《恶之花巴黎的忧郁》（钱春绮译。北京：人民文学出版社，2020年）

诗的本质和诗的灵魂。而诗性散文（poetic prose）虽然也拥有绚丽的修辞，但它最终目的总是为了传达作者的思想，诗意只是其逻辑形式之一种，散文诗，则是一个完满自足的世界，没有其他的目的。

文学的基本样式包括戏剧、诗歌、小说和散文，几乎成为一种常识，为人所共知。但换一个角度，换一个标准，就会想到另外的体裁。比如对话式的、讨论式的、警句式的等等。就后者而言，古希腊时候就不少，后来尼采又做了发挥，虽是只言片语，却意深境远。散文虽是一个看起来最少具有艺术质地的文体，它的体裁也不易泾渭分明，但却是多用途的，是最日常的，也是最能触及心灵的。培根、蒙田的散文众所周知。培根在哲学上很有建树，是历史上的中流砥柱之一，他的随笔，短小，零散，状似试笔，却警句迭出，屡屡被文学文集收入。蒙田随笔体量更大，视野更宽，论食人部落、论西塞罗、论寿命，俨然一幅全人类从外在到心灵的画像以及作者自画像。

从历时的角度看，诗歌在散文化。同时，它们之间又难分难舍，互为包容，互为映照，因而，散文诗的出现，也就水到渠成，顺理成章。散文诗正是诗与画的两栖同体。散文与诗的两栖，虽不可以做史诗那样的大事，却也可以成为一种艺术的载体。散文诗善于表现即兴、深沉的感情，微妙、多重的思绪，看起来像是一首诗歌将成而未成的样子，描述的是诗意的积聚过程。散文和诗，是写作上的技术分类，散文诗则更是一种鉴赏与批评。

波德莱尔强调他的散文诗是受了贝特朗的影响，贝特朗是法国浪漫派的小诗人，他留下的散文诗集《夜间的伽斯帕尔》却是法国诗坛上的第一部散文诗集，在形式上，每首诗分成五节或六节，每节中的诗句，不用脚韵，却有无形的韵律；在风格上，用造型的、绘画的方式将古风物在幻想中复活，所以，他把自己的散文诗称为"仿伦勃朗和卡洛画风的幻想诗"。在散文的流沙上建造诗的城堡。波德莱尔之后的象征派诗人如马拉美、魏尔兰都曾从事这个新的诗歌体裁创作。由于散文诗有内在的节奏和旋律，其音乐感并不亚于格律诗，有时反而胜过格律诗，同时又可以让诗人更自由地处理，因此在法国的诗歌领域里，散文诗一直是诗人们乐于采用的体裁。

纪伯伦曾赴巴黎学习艺术，其散文诗的写作当属自然而然的留学成果。不仅如此，我们会想，为什么是纪伯伦的散文诗赢得了世界第三的美誉（仅次于莎士比亚和我国的老子），受到如此的欢迎？简单来说，是因为他在传统和革新的结合上超越了上述这些诗人和作家。

# 二

纪伯伦（1883—1931），黎巴嫩的文坛骄子，就是这样一位诗画俱佳的艺术天才和优秀散文诗作家。事实上，纪伯伦的绘画比他的诗文更早地受到外界关注和扶持。1908—1910年间，他在巴黎学习绘画和雕塑时，大师罗丹就对他褒扬有加，称他是"20世纪的威廉·布莱克"。纪伯伦也确实以布莱克为榜样，常为自己的诗作画插图，可谓是，歌咏之不足，故手绘之。绘画和写作就是他的两条生命线。他的诗是浪漫主义的、隐喻性的，万事万物都可信手拈来，当作说教的材料，思想的载体；他的画则是象征主义的，充满神秘色彩，万事万物皆混沌一片，是天地初开的样子。他为《先知》所作的十二幅插图，画作的中心都是各样姿势的人体，眼睛永远是闭着的，更像是中世纪纯洁又虔诚的人类。如果说纪伯伦的诗文是站在了20世纪新文学的前沿，举起了阿拉伯新文学的大旗，他的绘画，则可以说并没有站到20世纪初痴迷于研究色彩和线条的印象派、后印象派或立体派、野兽派的行列。就像王维一样，虽然诗画兼善，第一把交椅也只能二选一，王维是画，纪伯伦是散文诗。

纪伯伦一生穿梭于东西方两个世界，既饱饮地中海和大西洋之水，又惯看黎巴嫩的雪松和北美榆树，文化浸润丰富，且天纵英才。纪伯伦不仅是一个诗画双栖的艺术家，更是一个双语诗人和作家，出版过八部散文诗集，其他尚有诗歌、诗剧、小说、散文和书信等传世，是20世纪阿拉伯新文学运动的先驱，黎巴嫩的文化英雄。作为东方弱小民族的文化英雄，纪伯伦与印度的泰戈尔一样受到我国读者的尊敬和喜爱。他的散文诗《先知》篇幅不长，如果以史诗为传统的标准论，算不上惊天动地或者惊世骇俗的巨著，然而，它赢得了超过荷马和弥尔顿的声誉，受到更多人的喜爱。早在1923年，茅盾就向国人译介了纪伯伦的散文诗。1930—1931年间，冰心完整地翻译并出版了纪伯伦的《先知》，并在其后多年间不断再版。

该散文诗集初版于1923年，正值纪伯伦文学创作的鼎盛时期，诗集用英文写成，在纽约出版。在此之前，纪伯伦曾出版散文集《疯人》(*The Madman*，1914)，表达了对尼采超人哲学的尊崇。虽然在形式、风格上，《先知》集与尼采的《查拉图斯特拉如是说》仍有异曲同工之处，都以先知为代言人，都作为一个陌生人生活在异地，都要告别世人回到自己的出生地或幸福岛，都在告别众人前为众人讲经，但是，二者的语调不同，两位先知对待世界和信众的态度也不同，显然，1923年的纪伯伦已经走出了尼采的阴影。在尼采的先知眼中，大海做着噩梦，先知怨恨着他自己："听啊！听啊！它是怎样在作着不愉快的回忆而呻吟！或者怀着不愉快的预期？／唉，我跟你一同忧伤了，你这黑沉沉的怪物，而且为了你，还怨恨我自己。／唉，我真恨我的手没有足够的力量！说真的，我真乐愿把你从噩梦中解救出来！——"①而纪伯伦的先知眼中，大海是母亲，是安宁，是自由，诗人要与大海融为一体："你啊，无穷的大海，不眠的母亲！／你独自成为大河溪涧的安宁和自由，／这溪流再蜿蜒一次，再在林中空地呢喃一回，／我就朝你奔来，一颗无穷的水滴，奔入一片无垠的汪洋。"②

　　事实上，《先知》读起来是一个有一定连贯的诗集，它的结构构成了一个完整的"故事情节"，很像亚里士多德所说的完整的故事（complete whole），场景和定位在海边、城市，文体形式是对话。如果就诗歌的规模、气势、主题而论，它有和史诗如出一辙的结构，具有宏大的规模，浩瀚的气势，主题涉及一些重大的命题，深度和高度都

---

① ［德］尼采:《查拉图斯特拉如是说》（钱春绮译。北京：三联书店，2007年），第174页。
② ［黎］纪伯伦:《先知》。除特别说明外，皆引自罗益民所译的本诗集，以下不再说明。

有些不同凡响，对话形式又使之显得亲切，如同拉家常，说闲话一般。这些因素有可能就是为什么读者觉得贴心和同心的理由，也是因为这些因素，他的诗集，才大受欢迎，赢得了排行第三的惊人的"桂冠"。

先知艾勒—穆斯塔法，上帝的选民，受到爱戴之人，时代的曙光，在奥菲利斯城里待了十二年，等待他的航船，把他送回到他出生的小岛。临行前，他和信众一起来到神殿广场前，在女先知阿尔米特拉和众人的发问下，先知给信众讲解人世上生与死之间的种种纽带和束缚。譬如，爱情，"像玉米捆一样，他把你收集到自己的身上。/他把你脱粒，让你赤身露体。他用筛子筛你，让你从壳儿中解脱出来。/他把你磨成白色的粉末。/他搓揉你，把你变软；/然后他把你架到他的圣火上，让你变成神的圣餐中神圣的面包"。又比如，友谊，"除非为了让精神更为深邃，友谊不要有别的目的。/因为只寻求揭露自身秘密的爱不是爱，而只是撒下的一张网，网住的都是些毫无用处的东西"。

艾勒—穆斯塔法的语言喻义丰富，充满张力，既有似非而是的悖论，又如雅典娜神庙里的谜语一般，深奥，多义。谈话涉及人生、哲学、美德等方方面面，就对话体而言，特别像柏拉图的对话录，或者孔子的《论语》，但又不仅仅是一个民主的交谈，而是先知占了主导，这些对话里又包含着环抱式的对话，特别让人想起《圣经》里西奈山上神对摩西的嘱托，但纪伯伦的先知显得更平等而贴心。

纪伯伦之所以选择散文诗作为他的表现样式，既源于他的留法经历，也源于当时他对西方现代文学的接受和对阿拉伯传统文学的改良。阿拉伯传文学统中的散文与诗歌都非常发达，前者原本就具有高度隐喻性、修辞性和程式化，极具诗性和艺术性，比如前伊斯兰时期占卜者的神谕话语、《古兰经》，以及伊斯兰黄金时期阿拔斯王朝的散文都可见一斑。纪伯伦的方式可以说是"新瓶装陈酿"，形式是西方现代的、新式的散文诗，内容是东方传统的美学、哲学和宗教等。但是，如前所述，纪伯伦的《先知》，在主题、结构、气势等方面，具有史诗的特点，史诗的精神，再加上文字的笔力，思想的隽永，表达的高妙，读者所需情绪、诗意、史诗般的构建与气度，行云流水的哲学警句式表达，水乳交融在一起，才为它赢得了喜爱和赞扬。这些突破也许是为什么这部篇幅不大，却具有史诗气度的对话居然可以在世界读者中位列"前三强"的原因。1923年诗集出版以来，到2004年第140次重印居然销售300万册，一时洛阳纸贵，纪伯伦成为第一个在西方引起巨大反响的东方诗人。迄今，这部诗集竟然被译成了一百多种文字！这也再一次加强了"洛阳纸贵"的印象。

<h1 style="text-align:center">三</h1>

大凡经典都有三个表现：一是不断再版，二是不断重译，三是时常被引用。《先知》这部作品，显然符合以上三个特点。目前摆在我们面前的这部《先知》新译本，就能说明它的经典性。我虽绝没有藏书家的财力物力和眼光，但也难免文人积习，喜欢收集一些特别之书的不同版本或译本，比如，不同版本的《莎士比亚全集》，不同译本的《瓦尔登湖》，各种版本的《石头记》或《红楼梦》等。关于纪伯伦，手中有他的英文版文集、传记和各种汉译本，林林总总十来种，是我热爱的诗人之一。因此，我也非常重视《先知》这部名著，同时关注诗集的中译本。因为译文本身，也是诗美存在的一种方式。

杨周翰先生说过，翻译是一个解释的过程，译者往往本能地要把原文晦涩难懂的地方译得使人能看懂。这样一来，译文往往比原文明澈。译本除作为一种美的形式，也是一种解释的形式和一种学习的形式。我有幸在出版付梓前读到罗益民教授的新译本手稿，对我来说，既是一种审美，也是一种学习。罗益民教授是在文学、美学和翻译界均深耕勤学的学者、专家和译者。他学识渊博，文采风流，著作等身，由他来新译《先知》，正是适得其人，恰逢其会。我作为第一个读者，只从我的见识、能力和理解的角度谈谈我的一些收获和看法。

一般来说，评论译本，均从公认的翻译原则和标准来说。大家说一不二的传统首要标准是"信"，或者它的同义词，如"忠实""等效"。我也是一个译者，也译过一些作品和篇什，因此，关于"信"作为首要标准的问题，我是完全同意的，因为我有感同身受的实践做依据。

可以看出，罗老师对待翻译的第一要求就是"信"，就是要在原作的形式和内容方面都尽量达到忠实于原文。这一点不仅从他的译文可以看出，在他给目前这部诗集写的序里面，也可以看出。罗老师关于"等效天平"以及"内在语法结构"，新批评的读诗原则及其在翻译实践中的应用，都表明他对翻译原则所持的态度。

他认为，"信"这个标准不仅是中国译学界的共识，也是世界范围内无可非议的看法。然而，问题是，人们往往把"信"理解为语言学家索绪尔所谓的"所指"（the Signified）方面的意义，不包括语言在声音和符号等方面即"能指"（the Signifier）的特点，正是因为这个特点，人们对翻译过程中应该执行的标准参数就有遗漏，或者本着讨好读者的目的，移植原文，或者本着美化译文的目的，因韵害意，都使"信"的准则难于完全实现。

针对这个老大难问题，罗老师在译本序言中提到，他赞成人民文学出版社编辑、译著与著作等身的翻译家苏福忠先生的意见，将"信"分解为四个具体可操作和监测的标准，简称"四M"法：meaning（意义），information（信息），message（隐义）和image（形象），即在基本意义、上下文、隐含意义以及形象意义方面，表达出既分又合的意义总和，较之严复的"信、达、雅"更为具体化<sup>①</sup>。罗老师认为，这特别像美国"新批评"学派创立的一个表达意义的词，Tension。这个词看似与已有的tension（张力，即同时存在的向两个相反方向伸张的力）相同，它的实际意义却是形式与内容意义的总和，或所指与能指意义的总和。苏福忠先生提出的四个M之说，是把新批评的Tension这个词的具体含义以及严复、刘重德甚至持等效观点的批评家们和理论家们提出的宏观指导和翻译原则，苏福忠先生则具体而微地落到了实处，提供了解决这个问题的方法。

以此为准则，作为莎士比亚戏剧与诗歌的研究专家、

① 苏福忠：《说说朱生豪的翻译》(《读书》2004年第5期)，第23—31页。

编辑家和翻译家，苏福忠先生细读、钻研、比对朱生豪翻译的莎士比亚戏剧及其原文，发现朱生豪所提炼出来的口语化译文，与莎剧的文字风格最合拍，译文表达力最强，符合剧中各类人物的身份，同时，朱译中大量的诗体译文，也十分珍贵，是译者用改革的旧体诗，翻译莎剧中的散诗的极好尝试，达到了英汉两种文字互相"移植"中的空前吻合。苏福忠先生还收集相关译例，进行比对。通过常年的编辑经验和自己的翻译实践，苏先生总结出了他从语素、语词到篇章的理论，汇成上述四条标准，也通过他收集的译例，来测试和检验这四条标准。罗老师的新译，或许可以说，是对苏福忠四 M 说的一个实践的田野例证。

## 四

纪伯伦《先知》集的语言与风格最大特点是，单词和句子均衡而对称，惯用排比，回环复沓，思绪连绵，情感堆叠，自成韵律，犹如海浪，一波未平一波又起，中间夹杂着激问和呼告，层层推进，形式与内容浑然一体。纪伯伦总是在第一句提出话题，接着进行平行列举，然后再从反面进行列举，最后重新提出话题，得出结论。在结构上，就像一首拉长、放大了莎士比亚十四行诗，起承转合，秩序井然；在形式上，则是多声部的，有交响乐和狂想曲的效果。正是这种雍容起伏的音乐感，使纪伯伦的先知读起来不似智者的说教，更像一位思想深邃的浪漫主义者的抒情，因此更能深入人心。

诗集的语言是平易的，但是又是用诗的比喻、意象表达的，其中的道理用诗化的语言、比方和象外之象来表达的。用一句中国话来说，常常是"境生象外"。译者坚持的"信"的原则，是包含形式和内容的信息的不折不扣，"原封不动"的再现。这样的文体，把大致意思表达出来，是人人努力做，而且也容易做到一定程度的。尤其特别的是，《先知》是准史诗式的散文诗，如果形式再现打了折扣，就很容易落入纯散文的窠臼。

在译法上，如果仅仅是亦步亦趋，可能把外显的形式译出来了，灵魂深处的那种暗藏的形式又会丢掉。所谓信不等于僵死的硬译或欧化，也绝不是周作人所说的"欲求信反而不达"，亦非常说的"亦步亦趋"，而是全方位从里到外，从内容到形式，与原文尽力保持最短的距离，最少的偏差。这一点也是新译本译者的原则和期待。罗老师在他的序言论文中多次阐述了这个观点，在这个《先知》译本与同步的泰戈尔的《园丁集》的翻译中，都践行了这个原则和观点。

新译《先知》行文严谨，诗意浓郁，恬淡超逸，形意和合，正好体现了译文对原文之"信"和诗意之传达。译本基本上在这三个方面都是成功的。第一，在基本意思上，力求不多不少不加不减不折不扣，在语序句法上不随意变换句式，这些都是原作表达意思和情绪的基本要素。比如"谈爱情"一节里的三处：

And when his wings enfold you yield to him,

Though the sword hidden among his pinions may wound you.

他展开翅膀，把你拥住，你便听从他摆布吧，

哪怕那把藏在他羽毛中的剑也许会伤着你。

And when he speaks to you believe in him,

Though his voice may shatter your dreams as the north wind lays waste the garden.

他对你说话，你就相信他吧，

哪怕他的声音，会使你的梦破灭，正如北风会让花园成为一片荒芜。

For even as love crowns you so shall he crucify you. Even as he is for your growth so is he for your pruning.

因为即使爱情为你加冕王冠，他也还会把你钉上十

字架。即使他栽培你，也还会把你修剪。

这样的处理方法，绝不是欧化和翻译腔。从译文可以看出，行文是充分考虑了读者的接受审美期待的。第二，在基本意思正确的情况下，译出原作的气度、韵味和灵魂。比如，

The soul walks not upon a line neither does it grow like a reed.

The soul unfolds itself, like a lotus of countless petals.

灵魂不在一条直线上行走，也不像一根芦苇那样成长。

灵魂把自己展开，就像荷莲，有无数的花瓣。

这每一句读来，都充满诗意，也朗朗上口，像名言警句一样让人难以忘怀。第三，就是在基本意义与形式意义俱有的时候，读起来畅达，不见斧凿之形，把"新批评"叫做 Tension（"合义"）的全部内容整体上再现出来了。这一点读一段离开原文的"译文"就清楚了：

除开业已半睡半醒地躺在知识的晨曦之中的，谁也

不能向你揭示什么。

　　行走在庙宇的阴影之中，和他的追随者一起的老师，给的不是他的智慧，而是他的信仰和怜爱。

　　倘若他真的很明智，他便不会让你走进智慧的殿堂，而是领你走向你自己心灵的门槛。

　　天文学家可能会向你说起他对宇宙苍穹的理解，可是他给不了他的理解。

　　音乐家可以对你唱出广袤苍穹的节奏，但他给不了捕捉节奏的耳朵以及回应那回音的嗓子。

　　谁精通数字的科学，就可以讲说重量和尺度的领域，可是他无法引领你走向那里。


　　以上管中窥豹式的调查，让人感觉尝鼎一脔可知一镬之味，睹一叶而可以知三秋之色，译本精彩之处不胜枚举，完全可与原文媲美。译文好，得益于译者坚持的原则，据此原则所做的努力，他自己的能力有多好。就这个译本而言，译者一贯坚持的原则就是，译文要到达的效果就是"信"，从里到外的"信"。一个译本是否忠实地体现了原文，关键就在这一点上。虽然这个观念是古老的，于翻译本身来说，却是基本的，而且是永远基本的。如何与原文保持最近的距离，读者可以自己去阅读，去体会。读者也可以甩开译本品味原文最好，若不能，则在译文中去找原作的风采和精神。好的译文总是能最大限度上体现这些特征的，尽量少地丢失弗罗斯特所说的"翻译中丢失的东西"，我也希望读者和我一样，满足了这个美好的期待。

译文美与不美，在这样的话语平台，也不可能穷尽，不可能一个一个地去阐释，再说，作为众多读者之一，我的理解也只能是一种管见和己见。最终的权力，还在所有的读者的手中。我只起一个抛砖引玉的作用，做个向导而已。美丽的风景，最终还得看风景的游客自己去体会。

总之，一个新的、可靠的、有很好质量的译本诞生了，这是一件美好的事情，是一件令人欣喜的事情，这也意味着，一个新的阅读行程又要开始了。